Amanda Dark meets a ghost...

She froze when from a corner of her left eye she saw movement. Looking down she saw a black cat with a white tipped tail padding across the room on its paws. Unable to look away Amanda watched the cat until it vanished into the wall.

Her heart beat hard in her chest and she sucked in a breath. The cat hadn't been real, at least not anymore. It was a ghost.

Amanda had seen strange things but never an actual ghost. Most of the paranormal activity she'd witnessed was minor stuff, objects moving by themselves, sudden fluctuations in room temperature, mysterious breezes on a calm night, and things that go bump in the night. She'd never seen a real, live ghost. Uhhhh... correction, a real dead ghost.

Amanda let her head sink back to the pillow and closed her eyes. *I must be seeing things...*

"Hello, Miss Dark?"

Amanda's eyes popped open and standing at the side of the bed was a square jawed man, his chin and cheeks covered in dark stubble. His jet-black curly hair was cut short and his eyes were as blue as a Caribbean sea. His lips formed a wry smile and his eyes twinkled.

"Uhhh...yeah...I'm Amanda Dark." Her brow wrinkled as she eyed the man. "Are you Phillip Swann?"

Love Stories

Russ Crossley

Cover art: © Suprijono Suharjoto | Dreamstime.com

ISBN 978-1-927621-41-7

Logo image by:

Engraver | Dreamstime.com

Published by 53rd Street Publishing
www.53rdstreetpublising.com

Table of Contents

Introduction

Hook Island

A Bad Day in Lunden Texas

One Red Shoe

Big Hairy Deal

Grind Manor

About the Author

Other titles by the Author

Introduction

Many readers of romance enjoy erotic elements in their stories. While I respect those authors choices to go in this way, this is not the kind of romance fiction I enjoy reading or writing. I write and read more traditional romance where true love is the catalyst that drives the story. I may be a romantic but I still believe true love lasts far longer than animal attraction. Having been married to my true love for almost thirty years I can personally attest true love can and does exist and does last.

I hope you enjoy these five stories and welcome feedback on Facebook or my website at http://www.rghart.com.

Hook Island

AMANDA HELD OUT THE FLASHLIGHT, but the muddy beam of white light barely penetrated the inky, thick darkness more than a few feet. ahead. Her heart beat loudly in her ears as she carefully stepped forward on the rickety wooden dock. She glanced over her left shoulder to see Pierre in the launch he'd used to bring her to this isolated island off the coast of South Carolina. She swallowed hard and for the hundredth time doubted she'd made the right decision.

"Pierre!" she called. "Which way?"

Squinting into the impenetrable darkness Amanda could just barely make out a man's shape bathed in the glow from the instruments in the dash of the boat. Pierre was at first understandably reluctant, but once she flashed a hundred dollar bill he readily agreed to transport her to Hook Island.

Hook Island

The transplanted Cajun, originally from New Orleans until Hurricane Katrina, was amiable and friendly during the ride from Isle of Palms. She sensed he thought she had a screw loose, but if anyone told her she'd make such a trip in the dead of the night, she might have agreed with him.

"Straight ahead!" she heard his voice echo over the sound of the rhythmic waves.

Amanda swiveled her head back and forth still unable to see her way along dock. Night vision wasn't her best feature. A strange skill not to have when you're a paranormal investigator since she often worked at night. Her breathing was rapid and her mouth and nose were filled with the smell of wet sand, salt air, and the acidic odor of rotting seaweed. "Too bad I can't lose my sense of smell on command," she mused under her breath.

As she carefully moved one foot ahead, the boards creaked. If she didn't walk off the edge of the old dock no doubt it would collapse beneath her.

She should have come in the daytime, but the letter said it was a matter of life and death. She had seen enough ghosts to know death intimately so she dropped everything back home in Boston and caught the first plane to Charleston.

Of course, the certified check for five thousand dollars certainly added to her motivation to come quickly.

Such a large amount of money as a deposit surprised her until she did some research on the plane using her IPad. According to the websites she surfed her mysterious benefactor, Phillip Swann, was a descendant of the notorious pirate, Captain Henry "Blackblood" Swann who sailed these waters in the mid 18th century. Captain Swann pillaged French, British, and Spanish ships for valuables, slaves, coffee, and anything else of value. Legends told he once captured a ship then set the crew adrift in lifeboats before setting fire to their ship. This last part of the legend was unconfirmed, but if true then Swann wasn't as despicable as many of his contemporaries.

Her problem right now wasn't proving the truth behind the musty legend, it was surviving the trip from the dock to the Swann family house somewhere on this speck of sand and rock. She'd survived worse, but not being able to see where she was going in pitch blackness had always been her greatest fear.

The light from her flashlight flickered twice then went out. Just great, she thought. Now what I am gonna do?

Hook Island

She stuck the tip of her tongue out one side of her mouth and concentrated on her footing. She then took one step and heard a crack as her foot dropped through a hole in the boards. Oh, oh. Not good.

Finally extracting her foot she lost her balance and stumbled forward. She lost her grip on the small suitcase in her right hand and it flew away from her to be lost somewhere in the darkness. A twinge of relief came over her when she heard it land on sand. At least her extra blue jeans, shorts, and tops would be dry. And her IPad and cell phone would still function. Salt water destroyed electronic gear thoroughly and quickly. Without her equipment her trip to Hook Island would have been pointless. If there was a ghost she would need photographic evidence. No photos, no future book, no future book, no food on table. Girl's gotta eat.

Knowing she was about to fall off the dock she held out her hands, closed her eyes ready to break the inevitable bones. Hopefully she wouldn't break anything important. She fell forward and found herself sprawled face down on sand. Her mouth had filled with the stuff and she spat out the sticky grains as best she could but the annoying grit was stubborn and wasn't going without a fight. She'd never liked the beach. There was too much sand, too much wind, and too much salt water for her liking.

When she tried to lift her head dizziness gripped her accompanied by a wave of nausea. She set her head back on the sand. The feelings passed but she realized there was a half buried stone in the sand sticking up. She must have struck her forehead against it. A growing warmth pooled around her head confirming her theory she was bleeding. The unmistakable odor of blood flooded her nostrils. Oh, crap. So not good.

She suppressed the urge to cry. I'm going to die on a desert island, in the dark, alone. She investigated the paranormal, she didn't want to be part of it, at least not yet. I'm too young to die.

The panic gripping her finallyfaded replaced by rationality. I need to stop wallowing in self pity, she scolded herself. Just because Paul left with the cat doesn't mean I have to fall to pieces during every tiny crisis. Oh, oh...as if a window closed Amanda's world abruptly disappeared.

***

Amanda's eyes fluttered open and through fuzzy vision came streaks of filtered sunlight across a wood ceiling. Her vision cleared and she shifted her head to her left.

She saw a window framed by shredded curtains. The glass in the window was missing so a breeze made the curtains move and billow like torn rags in the wind.

Shifting her legs she realized she lay on her back, her head rested on a severely squashed pillow. The air reeked of dust and mildew. Her mouth was devoid of moisture. She ran her tongue over her dry lips then gradually raised up on her elbows until she sat up. She blinked and her dry eyeballs clicked.

Her head throbbed. Instinctively she placed one hand on the side of her head and her fingers brushed a bandage wrapped around her wounded noggin. Now she recalled the fall at the dock. It must have been a while ago since it wasn't night anymore as evidenced by the sunlight creating a spotlight effect on the dirty wood floor.

She froze when from a corner of her left eye she sotted blurry movement. Looking down she saw a black cat with a white tipped tail padding across the room on its paws. Unable to look away Amanda watched the cat until it vanished into the wall.

Her heart beat hard in her chest and she sucked in a breath. The cat hadn't been real, at least not anymore. It was a ghost.

Amanda had seen strange things but never an actual ghost.

Most of the paranormal activity she'd witnessed was minor stuff, objects moving by themselves, sudden fluctuations in room temperature, mysterious breezes on a calm night, and things that go bump in the night. She'd never seen a real, live ghost. Uhhhh...correction, a real dead ghost.

Amanda let her head sink back to the pillow and closed her eyes. *I must be seeing things...*

"Hello, Miss Dark?"

Amanda's eyes popped open and standing at the side of the bed was a square jawed man, his chin and cheeks covered in dark stubble. His jet-black curly hair was cut short and his eyes were as blue as a Caribbean sea. His lips formed a wry smile and his eyes twinkled.

"Uhhh...yeah...I'm Amanda Dark." Her brow wrinkled as she eyed the man. "Are you Phillip Swann?"

He nodded. "You really didn't have to come out here in the middle of the night."

She cringed inside. He was correct of course, but for some reason she sensed he needed her as soon as possible. She had no idea where the sense of urgency came from, just that it had. "You're right, of course, Mr. Swann."

He chuckled. "Mr. Swann was my father. Please call me Phillip."

His smile disappeared and he arched one eyebrow sending a shiver of longing through her. She had never had a steady boyfriend since high school, when immediately after the grad party Dave Allister announced he was going back east to college and broke up with her. He broke her heart. That was of course after they'd had sex for the first time.

Since then she'd been on a few dates but nothing stuck. Of course after college she'd become a paranormal investigator. Men didn't seem to like women who chased dead things. When Paul left he made that much clear.

"Hello, Phillip," she held out her right hand which he grasped lightly in his as they shook hands. His warm gentle touch sent shock waves of desire through her unlike anything she'd ever experienced not even with Dave in the back seat of his fathers Durango back in her high school days.

"I thought I'd better come as quickly as possible," she explained. "Your letter said it was a matter of life and death."

Phillip's cheeks glowed crimson, his eyes averted looking at her instead he looked in the direction of the window. He moved away to the window and gazed out at the rolling surf of the ocean beyond the few trees sticking up from the tan colored sand in front of them.

Amanda rose to a seated position and then swung her legs over the side of the bed. Her head throbbed but she ignored the pain. She came up behind him and detected a sense of sadness emanating from Phillip. For most of her life she'd had a gift of empathy. She couldn't read minds but had a strong sense of their feelings.

It certainly made her life interesting at times, and not always for the good. Back in high school she'd managed to avoid the bullies when she detected their bad feelings toward her. Of course it didn't hurt when your best friend Mary Olson, was captain of the lacrosse team. Mary was as tough as any boy and had been known to flatten a few.

Amanda placed a hand on Phillip's shoulder. He jerked his shoulder away from her touch as if her skin were on fire. "Sorry," she whispered dropping her arm to her side she waited.

He turned to face her. He forced a thin smile on his lips. "I'm sorry, it's just my wife..." His voice trailed off and his next words caught in his throat.

"I'm sorry, I didn't know you're married." She sensed his sadness. "Did she die or something?"

Phillip watery gaze locked with hers. "No. She's alive and living in Alaska. With my ex-partner."

Amanda wondered if maybe she'd tread on forbidden ground.

"Sorry. It's none of my business. I —"

"It's okay, Miss Dark. You're empathy is a gift. Yes, I know about your ability to sense feelings. I wondered if it were true when I hired you. I can see it is, maybe a little too true."

Amanda raised both eyebrows. "What do you mean?"

"My wife left me ten years ago. We were high school sweethearts but after that it became clear our lives were on different paths. I still care about Julie, but we've both moved on."

Testing of her abilities was expected so Amanda wasn't insulted or annoyed. Honestly if she was in a client's shoes she would doubt her as well. When you say it out loud a woman who chases ghosts for a living sounds like rubber room time. "Are you married now?" She winced. "Sorry, that's really none of my business."

Phillip laughed. "No worries. I'm just glad you're here." He arched an eyebrow. "And, no I'm not married. Divorced."

Time to change the subject. "Did you see a cat?"

The sexy smile disappeared from Phillip's features. He frowned. "Cat? Was it black with a white tipped tale?" Amanda nodded. "And did it disappear out this window." He pointed to the window. "Or through a wall?"

Amanda's eyes widened. "How did you know?"

Phillip nodded. "Come with me into the old library."

Amanda followed him out of the bedroom into a musty hallway. The walked side by side to the end of the hall where there were double doors. The original brass handles now black with age lay on the floor where they had fallen as the doors rotted away.

Phillip pushed the doors open with one hand and they went in. The old library walls were covered in shelves of rotting books. The odor of decay was heavy in the air. At one end of the room sat a large ornately carved oak desk. On the desk was a hand carved wooden box about the size of modern briefcase. Only it clearly wasn't modern. The carvings depicted slaves harvesting tobacco leaves, and images of a sailing vessel with its sails bulging from the wind. There was also an image of a grinning skull over crossed swords, a classic motif for flags of the pirate age.

Amanda concluded the box had once been the property of one Captain Blackblood Swann, Phillip's ancestor. Her eyes flitted to Phillip then back at the box. Phillip certainly didn't look like a bloodthirsty pirate, and not like any of the ugly pirates in those Disney movies. Actually he looked more the pirates adorning the covers of steamy romance novels.

A sun warmed face turned nut brown, dark curls, and muscular arms clearly visible beneath his jean shirt, the top two buttons of which were undone to reveal a wisp of dark hair. His looks alone stirred her more than any man had in a long time.

Phillip moved to the desk and flipped the lid of the box open to reveal a well worn, leather bound book inside. A strong smell of leather filled the room. He gingerly lifted it from the box and set in flat on the desk. Carefully as if handling a baby he turned the yellowed pages to the middle of the thick volume.

Amanda stepped closer to study the odd writing. The words were written in the style of calligraphy, the words ornate and flowing. "What is it?" she asked.

"The diary of Captain Henry Swann."

Amanda's eyes widened. "Really? It must be old."

"Very," he nodded. "The pages are brittle with age so after we find the treasure I plan to donate the book to the Smithsonian."

Treasure? A frown creased Amanda's brow. I nearly kill myself thinking this is a life and death mission I'm only to find he's after gold and silver? Amanda wasn't rich, in fact she was on the low side of the middle class, but she wasn't a treasure hunter.

To her contact with paranormal phenomena wasn't about seeking lost objects, or obscene wealth, it was to help the dead achieve their just reward or at least be released from earth to go on their way. Sometimes they didn't appreciate her intervention but the living relatives often did.

"What's this about treasure?" she said, straining to keep the anger in her gut from her voice.

Phillip swiveled to face her. He offered her a lopsided grin. "Sorry, I'm not a treasure hunter if that's what you're thinking."

Amanda eyed him with one eyebrow cocked. Did he have her ability to sense emotions too? "What does his diary say?"

Phillip's shifted back to gaze down at the pages of the open book. "Captain Swann's diary says he had a cat. A black cat with a white tipped tail. It's name was Scars."

Amanda's eyes went wide and she stepped to his side her eyes on the pages. "Really? I saw a cat like that in my room..." Her cheeks grew warm. "Uhhh, I mean your room...uhhh...I mean the bedroom." Oh, crap he's gonna think I'm an idiot. All she wanted to do right now was crawl into a dark corner and die of embarrassment.

Phillip however didn't seem to notice her sudden discomfort.

His eyes were on the pages of the book. "Yes, I expect you saw the ghost of his cat."

Amanda shivered as a sudden coldness enveloped her accompanied by a feeling of dread. She's experienced feeling like these before during investigations in haunted houses, but never with this intensity. Her heart beat hard and time seemed to slow down.

A sharp movement at the edge of her left eye made her turn her head slightly toward the source. What she saw made her freeze and draw in a ragged breath. Her heart beat rapidly. A man dressed in pirate garb with a long saber dangling from his belt, his dark eyes scowling at her, his white frilly shirt stained with dirt stood eyeing her with one hand resting on the hilt of the sword. His free arm cradled the cat she'd seen earlier, it's white tipped tail flicking to and fro. Could it be a hallucination caused by the blow to the head?

"Uhhh, Phillip, do you see him?"

Phillip looked at her his eyes quizzical. "Who?"

Amanda pointed to where the pirate, with his three cornered wide brimmed hat sporting a black feather, stood silently watching them. Phillip scanned the spot she was pointing and shook his head.

"I don't see anything..." His words trailed off, his face became the color of ash. "A ghost," he whispered. His hands were trembling. "You see a ghost don't you?"

"Yes. At least I think I do."

"You mean you've never seen one before?"

Amanda swallowed hard as she placed one hand on his arm. She needed to steady herself before she collapsed. Her heart pounded hard in her chest and her armpits leaked like Niagara falls. Any second her knees would buckle and she'd give a sack of potatoes competition to the floor. "As strange as it sounds, no, I've never seen a live one....uhhh, I mean a dead one..." Her mouth clamped shut to stop herself before she shoved both feet into it.

"What's he look like?"

Amanda shifted her gaze to the pirate who eyed her curiously. He carried the cat to a chair across the room, sat down now petting the cat with his other hand. The cat curled it's tail lazily around it's body and looked very content. It's unblinking mustard yellow eyes watched her.

"Well, he's a pirate and he has a cat. He's sitting on the chair —"

"Sorry to interrupt, Amanda, but there aren't any chairs in here. Haven't been in about two hundred years."

"Actually, the pirate's sitting on one right over there..." Amanda nodded to the spot where the pirate sat watching her.

He wore a half smile on his lips now. Amanda's fear had dissipated, replaced by growing annoyance. He was laughing at her. She was the only one who could see him and he finds her predicament funny. Truthfully she'd find her hard to believe too.

"Listen, Phillip, if I tell you there's a pirate over there sitting on a chair then there is. I never lie. I don't know why I see him, or his cat, and he may be the first ghost I've seen in the fles — in person, but I am a paranormal investigator. It's my job. It's what I do." She wasn't sure the pirate was real but she wasn't about to let anyone think badly of her chosen profession. Too many people thought paranormal investigators were scam artists and charlatans. Until they needed her services.

Phillip held up his hands in mock surrender. "Ok, ok, I did check you out. I know you're a paranormal investigator and according to my sources you're a darned good one."

Amanda took a step away from him and eyed him with a scowl. "You checked me out. With whom?"

Phillip dropped his arms to his sides, rolled his eyes, and emitted a soft chuckle. "Trust me, Amanda it's nothing untoward I assure you. I'm a lawyer in Boston, where you also live, and I have a client who used your unique services a couple of years back."

"Do you remember Ollie Hardson?"

She did indeed remember Ollie, the man she dubbed the roamer because his hands often ended up in the wrong places like on her bottom at the most inappropriate times. She also recalled helping him remove the ghost of his dead Aunt Grace from his ancestral home. Of course, he then sold the old house to a developer for a small fortune. It's a strip mall now.

"You know, Ollie?" she said.

Phillip snorted. "Yeah. Real creep." He shook his head. "I did the legal work on the sale of house you cleared of his aunt's ghost. He told me all about it." He chuckled. "Never seen a guy so scared in all my life. His story reminded me of the ghost stories we used to tell around the fire at camp Woebegone when I was a kid. But if there was one thing about Ollie he convinced me the tale wasn't fantasy."

Maybe Phillip wasn't such a bad guy. If he was telling the truth. "Why don't you tell me what this is really all about?"

Phillip glanced at the watch on his left wrist. "I imagine you're hungry. Why don't we eat and I'll tell you all about it? And then if you don't want to help me fine, you can keep the money and I'll call for a boat to take you back to *Iles of Palms*, no questions asked. Deal?"

Amanda considered his words. Phillip Swann was growing on her. And he seemed trustworthy, for a lawyer. She nodded. "Deal." Her stomach rumbled. She looked at Phillip her eyes wide with horror. He laughed first, then she joined in.

Before they left the library Amanda stole a quick glance at Captain Swann still seated with Scars curled in his lap. He nodded when she passed him. His expression was pleasant. A pleasant pirate, who woulda thought?

***

Phillip surprised her when they went out the back door off the kitchen of the old house. The kitchen was beyond repair, every wood surface was cracked by wind and heat, the glass in the window frames were missing so there was nothing to keep out the inclement weather when winter storms brushed the island. Phillip explained the family home had been abandoned just prior to the civil war. Parts of the house were damaged when the Confederate army used the house as a headquarters from which to launch troops or ships against Union forces.

In an attempt to drive out the rebel army the Union navy bombarded the island just as they had nearby Fort Sumter, but never succeeded in dislodging the Confederate troops.

At the rear of the house, Phillip had erected a tent, and to create his own shaded area he'd tied the corners of a tarp to the trees ringing his campsite. In the center of the camp was a fire pit, a shallow pit dug in the soft sand and clay, a ring of large smoke blackened rocks with a stainless steel grate covered the pit. Off a tripod over the pit hung a steel hook with an old-fashioned cast iron cooking pot.

"Water?" Phillip asked waving her to a camp chair to the right of the fire pit. She nodded and sat in the chair. The air was rife with wood smoke. To the left of the tent was a pile of firewood.

He went to an orange cooler and took out two bottles of water one of which he handed to her before squatting next to the pit to light the fire. Soon a blue and yellow flame danced under the grate, the wood snapping and popping as the moisture in the wood was heated and expelled. A trial of white smoke disappeared into the sky over head.

Amanda broke the seal on the bottle and twisted off the cap.

After taking a long swig of the cool water she put the cap back on the bottle and placed it in her lap. "You seem to have been here for a while."

Phillip concentrated on nursing the growing fire. "Yeah," he said, "a while. I was waiting for you. I sent the letter two weeks ago." He shrugged. "I didn't know how long it would take so I may have over prepared."

The fire crackled brightly, the flames now licked the grate. Satisfied Phillip rose to his feet and moved to the cooler again. "Hotdogs okay?" Since tubes of mystery meat were one of her favorite food groups, Amanda readily agreed, but just as she did at home promised herself to eat better in future. He glanced at her and grinned. "Good. Mustard, ketchup?" Again she nodded.

Soon they were eating barbecue hotdogs in silence, the smoke from the fire permeating everything.

Amanda swallowed a bite of meat, bun, and the mustard-ketchup mixture. She broke the silence first. "What's in the treasure that you're so interested in if it's not gold and jewels?"

Phillip stopped eating and looked at her. His eyes were serious, she worried she may have offended him. "I'm hoping the chest buried somewhere on this island holds the truth about my famous ancestor."

Her curiosity aroused Amanda continued. "I gather there is a letter or document that will tell a different story about Captain Swann than the tales told in the history books?"

Phillip took a small bite of his hotdog and nodded. "Yes. I believe there is a letter signed by the Queen Anne of England affirming Captain Swann was an agent of the Queen in the Caribbean, raiding Spanish and French colonies and their ships to disrupt trade."

"That's very different than what's recorded about your ancestor." Amanda frowned. "Why does this matter so much to you now? Surely after three hundred years it doesn't really matter all that much does it?"

Phillip's face became a mask of determination, his jaw line taunt. He threw the remainder of his meal into the fire. The fatty meat flared and she could smell it charring. "Before my father died of cancer last year he made me promise to clear the Swann name." He stopped and looked into her eyes. She saw his eyes lose their hard edge and his shoulders relaxed. "Sorry. I must seem a little obsessed. I may be, but Dad always felt the reason Captain Swann's name was dishonored involved family land claims in England."

Amanda curled an eyebrow. "Land claims?"

"Yes. When Queen Anne died in 1714 King Charles I assumed the throne. He was German and had little interest in English affairs of state, those he left to Sir Robert Walpole. The Walpole's and the Swann's were not on the best of terms since the Walpole's wanted the Swann lands, and because of a love affair that ended badly between cousins from each family."

Sounds like Romeo and Juliet, thought Amanda. She took a bite of her hotdog, chewed and swallowed. "They didn't like each other, so what does this all have to do with Queen Anne's letter?"

Phillip shook his head. "Walpole had all copies of the letter destroyed and announced that the English navy would hunt down Captain Swann and hang him as a pirate, which they did in 1719. What Walpole didn't know was a single copy of Queen Anne's letter with the royal seal remained hidden on this island. Over the years we've tried many times to find it without success."

Amanda finished her meal and felt rejuvenated. She took a sip of water then said, "You want me to ask Captain Swann where the chest is hidden. Correct?"

"Yes."

"And I suppose there are jewels and gold buried with the document."

Phillip smiled. "I don't know. And frankly I don't care."

"But I do," said a deep male voice to Amanda's left. Looking to the row of trees where the voice came from she saw a tall, dark skinned man step out from behind a tree. Her heart froze. In his right hand he held a snub nosed pistol pointed at them.

Phillip chuckled. "Ahhh, yes, Jim Sweet, my former partner. How nice of you to drop by. How long have you been listening?"

One corner of Sweet's mouth curled upward. "Long enough to know you may have found the key to finding the treasure." He waved the gun at Amanda. "Her."

Phillip made a move to stand, but Sweet waved the pistol at him. "Don't move," Sweet said his eyes narrowing.

Phillip shoulders slumped and he remained seated. "OK, Jim, you win. What do you want?"

"I want this little lady to accompany me inside the house, talk the ghost into telling me where the treasure is hidden, and then I'll be on my way."

Phillip arched an eyebrow. "What about me?"

"I was thinking I'd dispose of you first, but if the captain won't talk to me I may still need you. So I'm going to tie you up and leave you here. If I need you I'll come back for you, if not..."

Jim left the rest to their imagination, not that it needed much imagination to see he was going to kill them both regardless of what happened. As the pirates used to say, dead men tell no tales.

If there was a treasure buried with the letter about Captain Swann it would be worth a fortune in today's money. People have killed for far less.

"You," Sweet pointed the pistol at her, "find a rope and tie him up."

Amanda looked to Phillip. He nodded and pointed to the tent. "There's a rope inside."

Amanda's face grew cold. They were going along with this man? Why?

Soon, after some instruction by Sweet, she had Phillip tied to the chair and his mouth stuffed with a piece of dirt stained cloth.

"Let's go," Sweet said his voice menacing, his eyes flat with no emotion. How did Phillip get hooked up with such a man, someone capable of killing in cold blood.

Amanda started walking toward the house followed by Sweet who had the gun pressed into her back. One thing her father insisted she learn before she left home to move to the big city was how to use and care for guns.

She didn't really like guns, but when someone has one pressed into your spine, knowledge could in handy. Six hours a week at a gun range for three months made a girl fairly proficient with firearms.

She entered the house and went immediately to the library where they'd left the diary open on the weathered desk. Amanda was disappointed to see the chair and Captain Swann with his cat were missing.

Moving to the book she pretended to be read it. Her eyes flitted to movement as Sweet came from behind to stand beside her. He had the gun pointing to the floor at his side. He didn't see her as a threat.

A small smile played across Amanda's lips. Once his attention was on the book she decided her opportunity would never be better so she reached for the gun and managed to grab it and twist it out of his hand before he could react.

Stepping away she raised the weapon and pointed it at Sweet's chest. A quick glance confirmed the safety was off.

Sweet regarded her with his dead eyes. "Go ahead," he said, "shoot." He took a step toward her and she instinctively took a step back.

One thing her father hadn't taught her was the killer instinct.

Shooting paper targets was very different from shooting a living person.

Her fingers gripping the pistol began to sweat. "Don't move," she said.

"I don't think you'll fire," said Sweet stepping closer. He raised one hand and slowly reached for the gun.

"Don't! I will you know..."

Sweet grabbed the barrel of the pistol and pulled it from her slick fingers. Amanda's heart sank. She'd failed them both. They were going to die.

Sweet smiled grimly. "Now stop this nonsense and talk to the ghost about the treasure." He pointed the gun at her forehead. "Right now." he growled, "Or I will shoot you, and I won't chicken out."

"Sweet!" It was Phillip's voice. Suddenly Sweet and the pistol were gone. At her feet lay the tangled mass of two men locked in combat.

Amanda backed up until her body was pressed against the wall, while watching the struggling men. Phillip landed a punch on Sweet's jaw,, his head snapped to the right. Bones crunched and she could see Philips knuckles were inflamed. Sweet grunted from the blow and his head snapped back. He raised the pistol, which miraculously he hadn't let go of when Phillip tackled him.

Gritting his teeth Phillip grabbed Sweets arm, twisted it hard backward causing the pistol to fly out of his hand. The gun struck the wall behind them with a thud, then rattled to the floor. Amanda considered going for the weapon, but if she tried she might be knocked to the floor by the two men fighting. The room was too small for her to maneuver around them. They leaped to their feet and circled each other warily. Sweet's eyes kept flicking from Phillip to the gun then back again. Phillip's attention was focused solely on his opponent.

Sweet's hands formed fists. He leapt forward and swung a fist hard at Phillip's head. Phillip ducked inside Sweet's intended blow and landed a hard blow to Sweet's solar plexus.

The air rushed from Sweet's lungs, he gasped clutching his belly as he stumbled backward. Phillip stepped forward, landed a punch hard on Sweet's chin. The man's head snapped around and he collapsed into a heap on the floor where he lay still, his eyes closed. It was over. Phillip had won.

He moved unsteadily on rubbery legs, his lip was bleeding. His left cheek sported a purple bruise that was already badly swollen. He dragged air into his lungs.

Amanda rushed to him. She wrapped her arms around him, partially to keep him from falling and partially to comfort him. She grasped him by his shoulders and studied his bloodshot eyes. "Phillip, thank you for saving me."

He gave her a weak smile. "No worries."

"Who is he?" She nodded toward Sweet laying unconscious on the floor.

"My former law partner," Phillip said.

Amanda's eyes went wide. "He's a lawyer? Would he have really killed us?"

"Oh, yes. He was convicted of murdering his wife, and his mother-in-law. And that was for one hundred thousand dollars in insurance money. A priceless treasure proved too much for a greedy creep like him." His eyes drooped at the corners. "I should never have told him about my ancestor, but I thought he was my friend."

A cold dread washed over her sending chills up her spine. Maybe it was emanating from Sweet or Phillip, but she didn't think so. After releasing Phillip he leaned in to the wall and watched her as she moved to the desk and opened the diary again. She looked back to the spot where she'd seen the pirate before, sure enough there he was seated as before on the chair with the cat in his lap.

"Hello, lass," he said. There was definitely an English inflection in his voice.

Amanda thought for a second or two she might faint. Not only had she seen her first ghost, but he'd just spoken to her.

"Uhhh...hello?"

Phillip frowned. "Who are you talking to?"

"He's here again."

"Oh. Quick before he leaves again, ask him where the treasure is hidden."

Amanda opened her mouth to speak, but the ghost rose from the chair his hand resting on the hilt of his sword, the cat dropped to all fours it's tail wagging. "Why should I?" he said.

"Is something wrong?" asked Phillip.

This go-between conversation could get complicated. She had to discover another way to get these two together. "Captain. I'm wondering if you will show yourself to Phillip." She indicated Phillip with a slight nod of her head. The ghost scowled. He didn't appear open to the idea. Perhaps if she shared some information about him the captain might be more agreeable.

"Captain. I'd like to introduce you to your great-great-great grandson, Phillip Swann. The ghost arched one eyebrow.

She'd tweaked his interest, but not secured his cooperation. Time to go for broke. She wondered if ghosts had traces of their human emotions remaining. She hoped so if not than this would fall flatter than the Soufflé she tried to make once in Home Ed class. "Before his father died he asked Phillip to clear his family name."

The ghosts eyebrows rose together and his dark eyes narrowed. "What trickery be this, lass? I am charged by the Queen herself to be her agent in these waters."

"That was three hundred years ago. You were betrayed by Lord Walpole who branded you as a pirate and had you hung in 1719." The ghost of Captain Swann ran one hand across his throat. She knew she'd triggered a buried memory, and not a pleasant one. She continued her explanation. "Lord Walpole had all copies of the letter destroyed expect the one you hid here on the island. In order to clear your name in the history books, we need that letter."

Captain Swann frowned then said, "OK, lass, the boy can see me now."

Amanda's eyes flicked to Phillip. His face was pale and his eyes wide. He indeed could see the pirate captain. She worried it might be too much for him especially in his weakened condition.

As she watched his features relaxed and his demeanor changed. His face became calm and his eyes reflected determination. "Captain Swann. Sir. I'm your great-great-great grandson, Phillip — "

The ghost captain interrupted him with a burst of laughter his features were now split by a wide grin. "Weren't ya listen to the lass here, boyo. She told me yor tale o' woe. Or should ah say my tale o' woe."

Phillip's eyes flitted to Amanda and his cheeks flushed crimson. "Yes, of course." He smiled weakly at her. "She's a special lady with special powers."

"Lad, if ya press the palm of yor hand six inches to the right of the corner where the two walls meet a hidden panel will open. Inside you'll find the letter from my Queen." With those words the captain faded then disappeared. Looking around Amanda saw Scars the cat had also disappeared.

"Wow. That was something," said Phillip expelling the breath he'd been holding in. "Do you still see him?" he said looking at Amanda. She shook her head.

"Let's see what's hidden in the wall," she suggested.

Phillip moved to the corner and pressed the wall as the ghost instructed. There was a soft click then as if it were on a hinge a portion of the wall from the floor to the ceiling swung inward.

The section was no more than six inches wide, not enough to hide a treasure chest that much was clear. Dust accompanied the panel opening. Amanda sneezed when the dust filled her nose.

"Bless you," said Phillip. He reached into the open panel and pulled out a four foot long tube-shaped leather case. It had a carrying strap on one side and the size and shape suggested it might contain a map.

Amanda's heart beat rapidly, she was anxious to see what was inside. Phillip carried it to the desk she followed. They stood side by side as he opened the top of the case and peered inside. A smile played across his lips which became a full blown grin.

"I see a document inside."

"Is it a map?"

"Yes, tell us, Phil is there a treasure map in there?"

Amanda froze and shut her eyes tight. Oh, crap, Sweet's awake. A soft click told her he had the pistol. They were right back where they started. Doomed.

"Well, well ya, scurvy dog, do ya think I'd let the likes o' you get the drop on me family?"

A bloodcurdling scream made the hair on the back of her neck stand at attention and sent shivers down her spine. The scream ended abruptly as if a tap had been turned off. Amanda opened one eye to steal a look at Phillip. He too had his eyes shut.

After several seconds of silence that seemed like an eternity Amanda decided to take a look. She opened her eyes and turned around.

There was no sign of Sweet, the captain, or his cat. All that remained was the pistol laying on the floor resting near the wall where their would be murderer must have dropped it. She tapped Phillip on his shoulder, he turned around.

"What happened?" he said.

Amanda shook her head slowly. "I have no idea. I've never known ghosts to interact with the living. Unless..." It couldn't be but it was the only sane explanation, if you could call the paranormal sane. She set her jaw and explained. "I've read about this, but have never met anyone who's seen it. And least anyone who's still alive."

Phillip looked at her in awe his eyes wide. She continued. "In 1891 a man named Simon Polson, a medium reputed to have been to the other side, reported that when ghosts feel threatened or when they're angered they can will themselves to touch and interact physically with the real world. Polson said it drained them and in some cases destroyed them, but if the ghost were powerful enough they could even drag the living into the spirit world.

The living would not be able to escape and would spend eternity neither living nor dead, in limbo."

Phillip shuddered. "Sounds horrible. Do you think that's what happened to Jim?"

Amanda nodded. "Yes, I think so. But as my mother used to say, he made his bed he has to lie in it."

She turned to the desk and picked up the map case. "If this is the letter then we need to take it to a museum to get it authenticated. Old documents will crumble unless they're treated with great care. Do you agree?"

"Yes, but I'm anxious to see the letter."

Amanda grinned. "Me as well, but we have to be patient."

Phillip offered her a lopsided grin which got her juices flowing again. "Perhaps you and I can work together once we get back to Boston. What do you think?"

Amanda wanted to see him again in the worst way possible. Or was it the best? She smiled to herself. "Well, Mr. Swann, since you saved my life I think we can arrange something, but I must insist you let me buy you dinner."

"Agreed." He held out his hand, she took it in hers and shook to seal their agreement. Reluctantly she let go.

Russ Crossley

"Let's pack up your camp and call for a boat. I'm sure Pierre wouldn't mind coming back for us," she said. Phillip nodded then took the leather case from her and walked out of the library into the hall.

A small movement to her left shifted her attention away from the doorway toward the wall. Scars appeared from the wall padded to her and rubbed his body against her legs emitting a gentle purring sound. She sighed. Not only did she have a new friend and business partner, but somehow she had adopted a ghost cat.

Amanda watched Phillip go and it dawned on her her life was headed on a new path. She might even have discovered a best friend and maybe more, hopefully much more.

A Bad Day In Lunden Texas

SHERIFF WILL SPEAR HAD HIS DUSTY, WORN boots resting cross-legged on his desk his concentration fixed on the cigarette he was rolling between his thick fingers when Julia Carpenter stormed into his office. She really had a head of steam on today. Her pasty face was flushed crimson and her normally gentle blue eyes practically spat fire.

She dropped the edges of her ankle length skirt as soon as the door to the sheriff's office slammed shut behind her. Will could see her brother slash bodyguard, Slim through the window facing the main street waiting outside on the wooden boardwalk with his back to them.

"Sheriff!" Julia spewed the word like he did chewing tobacco into the spittoon at the town saloon. "They're at it again!"

Will sighed inwardly then placed the now rolled cigarette on his desk and swung his boots to the floor. His chair creaked in the now steamy air. Julia smelled of flour and panhandle dust. Given the bakery was busy today and there was a stiff westerly breeze from that direction this morning it wasn't surprising. Every day the bakery was busy it masked the horse manure odor usually permeating the air. "Sorry, Miss Carpenter, I'm kinda busy just now. What have they done this time?"

He knew she meant Colonel Montgomery's family. Her father, Colonel Carpenter, and Colonel Montgomery's had been rivals as long as they'd both been raising cattle at opposite ends of the county. Frankly, if it weren't for these two ranchers the town of Lunden set in the middle of the county wouldn't exist, and he wouldn't have a job.

"Mr. Aimes at the telegraph office says he sent a telegram to Houston asking a Steve Ballew to come here for a job for the Montgomery's. Ballew has to be a hired gun." She crossed her arms over the swell of her bosom and glared at him as if daring him to say she was wrong.

Will had always thought she looked her most attractive when she so riled up. "How do you know he's a hired gun?" If Will knew him Aimes probably told her Ballew was a gunslinger.

As a fan of those dime novels, Aimes frequently told tall tales based on these wild stories to the rapt attention of the younger towns folk. This time he'd told one of his fanciful tales to the wrong person. Julia had a temper and the recent attempted murder of her father really had her in an ugly mood.

Rumors had been swirling for weeks the two colonels were trying to hire gunslingers to end their feud once and for all.

Colonel Montgomery had served in the Confederate Army, Colonel Carpenter had been an officer in the Union Army. They had both been in the last graduation class at West Point before the war broke out. No one knew for certain what caused the two men's rift and seething hatred for each other, but Will suspected something happened between the two men when the war between the states erupted. Something very bad.

Fifteen years later the two men were now the most successful cattle barons in Texas. And they had families. Lately though something had changed. Colonel Carpenter had grown increasingly obsessed with revenge and seemed to have lost touch with reality. He'd killed one of Colonel Montgomery's bulls and hung a sign round the dead animals neck reading, 'You're next, Montgomery'.

Will had been able to work things out between the two men using their children as intermediaries. Carpenter paid Montgomery five hundred dollars in compensation for the dead bull. It was how he'd gotten to know Elbow Montgomery and Julia Carpenter. Unfortunately, this temporary truce wouldn't last for long.

"OK, Miss Carpenter, I'll check it out." Her features eased slightly. "If he's a gun for hire I'll turn him around and send him packing if and when he gets here. You have my word."

Will already shot and killed two men reputed to be hired guns in the last six months, but he knew his luck would run out eventually. His deputy had been on the losing side of one such fight. This dispute would end badly for someone. Will, was determined not to be on the losing end. Keeping the peace had once seemed very easy, these days the work came with substantial risks.

Sometimes he wondered if he should have stayed in Boston at college where he studied Shakespeare, Defoe, and Thackery. But the expansion of the west had called him as it had many young men after the civil war. A sharp twinge in his lower back reminded him he wasn't as young as when he'd left Boston nine years ago.

Julia's scowl faded replaced by a tight smile. Her eyes said she was skeptical of him. Not that he blamed her, he was after all a sheriff bought and paid for by her father and Henry Carpenter's steak-on-the-hoof money. He had been bought and paid for and everyone in town knew it. The irony that he was as much of a gun for hire as any of these men heading for Lunden to make a quick buck had never been lost on him.

"Thank you, Sheriff. Send a wagon for me when Ballew arrives. I want to see him leave for myself." Will nodded and inwardly rolled his eyes. The Carpenter's were a blood thirsty lot. Julia well knew if the man was a gunfighter he'd be leaving Lunden in a wooden box.

Even if he managed to kill Will Julia's two brothers, Slim and Edgar,'d shoot him down. They weren't good shots they just sent a lot of lead flying in one direction simultaneously. Enough lead and an ambushed man (shot in the back in most cases) stood little chance of survival.

Julia left his office the glass in the door rattled as it closed behind her. Through the window Will watched Julia and her brother until they disappeared from view.

Will picked up the cigarette he'd rolled earlier from his desk and placed it between his lips. He eased back the chair and pulled a match from the left pocket of his vest.

He struck the match on the rough wood of the desk. Yellow and blue flame burst to life, which he used to light the tip of the cigarette. The tip glowed orange and he puffed once then shook the match out leaving a bloom of burnt sulfur in the air.

The leather gun belt around his waist creaked as he stood and walked to the hat rack near the door and snagged his black Stetson and set it on his nest of curly blond hair.

He swung the door open to the street and stepped out onto the boardwalk. Will adjusted the weight of his colt .44 caliber peacemaker in the holster on his belt and started down the boardwalk headed for the telegraph office at the end of the street in the train station.

It was nearing ten o'clock as he passed the saloon. Hank Archer had just opened for business and two customers nodded at him as they went in through the swinging door. The two hotels with their gambling halls farther down the street would be opening their roulette, poker, and faro tables in a couple of hours. Then the nightly bouts of drinking, gambling, and whoring would commence.

The cattle drive season was still two weeks away. Until then Will and his new deputy were going to be busy little lawmen.

Russ Crossley

Finally after tipping the brim of his hat to a number of wives with children in tow doing their shopping at the general store he neared the telegraph office housed in the railway station. He pulled his watch from the other pocket in his vest, he thumbed the catch and it snapped open. The train from Kansas City was due to arrive in another hour. Accordingly there were supply wagons lined up beside the track to accept delivery orders for Mr. Miller's general store, Mr. Bishops feed store, the saloon, and the hotels. The wagon derivers were no doubt inside getting a drink of cold water out of the sun. It was a hot day and a little shade was certainly welcome.

Will stepped inside the station entrance and to see the delivery drivers huddled around the rain barrel near the entrance to the station platform chatting amongst themselves some of them smoking. Will dropped his cigarette butt to the floor and stepped on with his right boot. He glanced at the telegraph booth but didn't see Frank Aimes. No doubt he was making sure the baggage cart was in place for passengers when the train arrived.

Every week it seemed more and more people were arriving in Lunden.

The town was growing in equal proportion to the number of head of cattle the Montgomery's and Carpenter's raised on their ranches every year. From what Will heard 1875 would be a record year for both ranches.

Will took off his hat and wiped his forehead dry with the sleeve of his shirt then put his hat back on his head. He then walked to stand behind the delivery drivers. "How ya'all doin', gentlemen?"

The men dropped into silence and one of the larger of the men, a guy named Will recognized as Stanton, turned to face him. His sun weathered face and dark eyebrows gave him the appearance of a Bedouin traveler Will'd seen depicted in a book during his college days.

"Hi, Sheriff, what can we do for ya?" His voice was deep and rumbled. He had a smoldering cigarette dangling from one side of his wide mouth. Stanton wasn't a bad sort. Will had only arrested him once on a drunk and disorderly charge. The circuit judge fined him five dollars.

"Stanton." Will nodded. "I'm lookin' for Frank. Ya seen him?"

Stanton turned his head slightly to the left and indicated the platform behind him. Will offered the man a thin-lipped smile. "Thanks."

Without responding, Stanton turned back to continue his conversation with the other deliverymen.

Will walked past them onto the raised area and immediately spotted Frank Aimes at the very end of the platform struggling with a large wheeled baggage cart. It had six shelves and was made of solid wood. Will concluded it had to be new given the wood looked freshly hewed and wasn't marred by repeated use.

Another sure sign the town was growing up. Will hurried to help Frank move the surprisingly heavy cart to the middle of the station platform. Sweat dripped from Frank's chin and they were both breathing hard when they finally had it where it would be needed.

Frank took a handkerchief from his back pocket and wiped his face and beck with it. "Thanks, Sheriff," he gasped.

Will removed his hat and wiped the sweat from his eyes with his shirtsleeve. "Sure, Frank. More'n happy to help."

They walked in silence to the office passing the deliverymen who didn't bother to acknowledge them as they passed. Will smiled to himself. No one likes the law when they want to be tearing up the town, but when they needed help they come a runnin'.

Will followed Frank into the telegraph office closing the door after them.

"I think I know why you're here, Sheriff," Frank said as he moved to sit in the chair behind the desk with the telegraph unit.

Will arched an eyebrow. "Really? Why do you think?"

Frank's green eyes locked with his. "I 'xpect Julia Carpenter came to see you about a telegram I sent to Houston. About hiring another gunslinger."

Will nodded. "One Colonel Montgomery asked you to send..."

The corners of Frank's mouth curled slightly upward. His hazel eyes narrowed. "That's not exactly accurate." Frank paused and walked away to the door. He opened it a crack and saw the gaggle of delivery drivers hadn't moved then returned to sit behind the desk. His voice lowered. "Colonel Carpenter not Colonel Montgomery is tryin' to hire a gunfighter."

Will could not hold back his surprise. He let a soft whistle escape between his lips. Julia lied to him, or she didn't know. "What did you tell her?"

Frank shrugged. "I told her the colonel sent a telegram and I told her who I sent it to. She assumed it was Montgomery, not her father."

If he knew how to work out the mechanics, Will's next move would've been to kick himself in the rear. How could he be so stupid?

Somehow, Colonel Carpenter had discovered his new deputy and the colonel's daughter were having a passionate love affair. In hindsight he should never have hired a Montgomery son as his new deputy. The day he'd dreaded had finally arrived. As sheriff he would be forced to choose sides, or the town would become a shooting gallery with him in the middle.

***

Before he left the telegraph office, Frank told him he'd received a response within two hours. Ballew would be on the noon train tomorrow.

Will stepped through the swinging doors into the smoky, boozy saloon. His hat was pulled low on his forehead to create a shadow over his eyes. If anyone planned to challenge him they would have difficulty seeing where his eyes were focused. A second or two of doubt can often provide an advantage.

"Hey, sheriff." It was Hank calling him from behind the bar. Hanks round, flushed face and cheery manner made him popular with the locals. Will liked the gregarious bar keep. Will nodded to a group of four men playing poker in the center of the room when they glanced in his direction. They avoided his gaze and turned back to their cards.

Will walked across the room to stand at the bar. He placed one booted foot on the brass rail that ran along the base of the wide, solid oak bar. He smiled easily, flicked his hat back off his forehead to reveal his eyes with one finger, and ordered a beer. He glanced to his left and saw his deputy hovering over a half empty beer glass his head down as if in prayer.

Will thought about a prayer, not only for young Montgomery, but for the whole town if this mess got out of control.

He looked away from his deputy to the table to men playing cards shrouded in the smoke from their cigars and cigarettes. He recognized them. The four were lead hands on Colonel Carpenter's spread.

One of the men appeared to be reaching under the table. Will shoulders tightened when he realized the man known as Black Pete was reaching for his gun. As casually as possible Will shifted his gaze back to Elbow then again to Pete. Elbow hadn't noticed the sudden growing tension in the room. Will looked at Hank who had noticed. His eyes were wide and his features had turned ash gray in color and he was breathing more rapidly.

Will indicated with a nod of his chin for Hank to get down behind the bar, which the bartender did.

He then slowly dropped his hand over the butt of his colt and wrapped his dry fingers around the ivory handle with his index finger around the cool steel of the trigger.

Pete suddenly sprang from his chair his hand on the butt of his revolver. The chair he'd been seated in slammed to the floor rattling across the wooden planks before it came to a stop. But before he could pull his gun out Will had his out and leveled at the center of Pete's chest with the hammer cocked. Pete's hands were trembling and his eyes shifted to his three playing partners who remained seated with their hands resting on their guns still in their holsters.

"I wouldn't if I were you, Pete," Will growled. "And you three better stay where you are," he directed at the table of men. Will had a sense of satisfaction when he saw the three men's hands drop away from their weapons.

Pete's nervous gaze focused on the barrel of sheriff's gun. "Huh, listen, sheriff, we got no quarrel with ya. We gots orders is all."

Will sensed movement to his left and out of the corner of his eyes caught a glimpse of Elbow standing beside him with his gun out covering the table.

"Well, Pete, it seems you're out numbered two guns to one. Why don't you and your friends here leave town right now before things get complicated."

Pete's hand slowly eased away from his own gun and his eyes drooped at the corners. Suddenly his hand flashed to his gun but before he could draw to fire Will'd ears rang when Elbow's weapon spat fire in two quick shots. As if in slow motion Will watched the bullets enter Pete's chest creating a puff of fabric and flesh and a spray of blood.

Blood continued to spurt from the two dark bullet holes, as Pete was knocked backward off his feet from the concussion. A grunt escaped his lips as he hit the floor then lay still his eyes open staring at the ceiling. He coughed once then emitted a soft sigh as air left his lungs for the final time.

The three men gathered around the poker table stiffened, their hands once again gripped the stocks of their guns. They appeared ready to fight it out. Dark scowls marred their unshaven features and their beady eyes flitted between them as if signaling to each other.

"Drop your gun belts," Will said between gritted teeth.

"You heard him," Elbow standing beside him. Will detected the acidic odor of burnt gunpowder.

"Yeah," came a voice from the direction of the bar. Will glanced over to see Hank standing behind the bar pointing a double barrel shotgun at the three men.

Will smiled to himself. "Com'on, gentlemen, I believe we have you outgunned."

One of the men began to slowly slide his revolver from the holster. A loud boom erupted and the floorboard beside the man's chair shattered. The man howled in pain having been sprayed with stray shot tearing up his left leg from ankle to thigh. The full blast would have severed the leg and torn up the bone, but Hank aimed to miss in order to make his point he meant what he said. The two uninjured men loosened their gun belts and let them drop to the floor at their feet. One of the men, his eyes locked on Will's reached over and released the wounded man's gun belt. It too thudded to the floor.

"Now slowly get up and move to face the wall, your hands over your heads, " Will ordered.

The men did as they were instructed, one man helping the wounded man. Will holstered his weapon. "Elbow, take these three to the jail, then get the doc."

Elbow herded the men out of the saloon using his revolver as incentive the echo of his boot steps soon disappeared.

Will would check on them later then ride out to Colonel Carpenter to explain why he arrested his lead hands. He didn't intend to lay charges, just to make his point that murder of his deputy regardless of his family name wasn't tolerated in Lunden. At least not while he was sheriff.

He grimaced. After tomorrow he might not be sheriff.

Will stood over Pete's corpse. "Hank, we need the undertaker." There had been far too many deaths in this war. It had to end, and he was just the man to end it.

***

The next day the buggy carrying Julia Carpenter arrived within three minutes of Will who rode his horse. Normally he'd walk from the office but something told him he'd need his horse today. Will tied Balthazar to hitching post in front of the station.

Colonel Carpenter arrived strangely unescorted driving the buggy. As long as he'd known him the Colonel he never went anywhere without armed guards. Will told them about Ballew's arrival on the noon train when he'd rode out to their ranch house yesterday afternoon. The Colonel only nodded. His eyes had a far away look in them.

Not a good sign to Will's way of thinking.

Will's ears still rang from the angry shouts when he explained how he'd arrested his men and that they would remain in jail until this matter between the two colonel's could be settled. Once the Colonel calmed down he agreed to a truce after Will dealt with Ballew. Both man let slip within earshot of Julia who hired Ballew, the colonel and Will only shared a brief knowing glance.

Will's lean muscular frame felt tight from the tension in the air. The sheriff took of his hat pulled a handkerchief from his pants pocket and used it to wipe his brow. The air was hot and humid today, worse than yesterday. His nose wrinkled due to the odor of manure in the still air. The sky was cobalt blue today with not a cloud marring the horizon. No wind meant stagnation.

"Sheriff," said a deep voice behind him.

Will stuffed the sopping handkerchief in his pocket placed his hat on his head and turned around. His brow wrinkled, gray-green eyes studied him, the thin gray mustache over the upper lip twitched. The Colonel was dressed in his usual black suit with a black vest over a white cotton shirt. A gun belt hung off his narrow hips. Will recognized the weapon in the holster. A Colt navy cap and ball. A good gun but dated.

His peacemaker used the newer cartridges. In an extended shoot out he could reload much faster than the Colt navy. Of course if Carpenter used his gun, like the highly skilled shooter he was, at close range Will'd be dead before his body hit the deck.

"Yes, Colonel. What can I do for you?"

"Where's your deputy?"

Will stomach muscles tightened. He didn't know how the colonel would react. He could lie but as the good book says the truth will set you free. "He's guarding the prisoners from last night."

The Colonel's scowl deepened. "I'll come by the jail later." His tone was low and menacing.

Will nodded then walked away headed for the telegraph office. He passed Julia who offered him a thin smile that made him more uncomfortable than reassured. The atmosphere was as thick and he felt as if he were trying to walk upstream with every step.

He entered the telegraph office to find Frank receiving a message. His normally flushed face was pale and his cheeks and forehead were bathed in sweat. Today was hot and humid, but no more than any other day in Lunden. The sour stench coming off Hank was adding anything positive to the room that much was clear. Something was wrong.

"What's wrong?" Will asked when Frank looked up as he slammed the door shut behind him.

Frank held up one hand. He was frantically scribbling on a pad of paper as the key clattered rapidly. Finally it fell silent.

"Ballew jumped from the train a mile back."

Will froze. "How long ago?"

Frank shrugged. His fingers wrapped around the pencil began to tremble. "They didn't say, but they haven't seen him for half an hour at least. The train's replenishing its boiler. They'll be here in twenty minutes."

Will's mind raced with possibilities. If Ballew was on foot it would take some time to get here, but if someone supplied him a horse he —"

His thoughts were interrupted by the sudden sound of repeated gun fire echoing through the station. Will pulled his peacemaker from the holster and signaled to Frank to stay seated. Frank nodded his lean frame shook so badly Will thought he might fly apart.

Will counted ten shots from two different weapons when the firing stopped. It must have lasted no more than thirty seconds, but it seemed to have been an eternity.

After moving slowly to the door, his gun held at the ready, the hammer cocked, he turned the doorknob and pushed the door open with the flat of his free hand. He peered toward the raised area and saw a single body sprawled on it's back. The body had on a dress and was surrounded by blood. The delivery drivers were nowhere to be seen. They hadn't been armed so he knew they weren't involved in the shooting.

Julia. She'd been shot. Will had seen his share of death, but seeing Julia unmoving, bleeding upset him more than he thought possible. He swallowed hard then slowly let out the breath he'd been holding since the flurry of gunshots rang out. He didn't see any signs of anyone else.

He curled his fingers tighter around the butt of his gun and flexed his arms. Stepping out onto the raised area crouching he sprinted across the platform until he reached the wall beside the entrance to the station platform. He had his back to the wall. Julia lay still in the middle of the open archway to the raised area her eyes were closed but her chest was rising and falling. She was alive.

Will edged to the entrance to the platform and once there he stole a quick look around the wall. No one was in sight. The air was dominated by the odor of gunpowder.

Will crouched down as much as his large frame allowed and moved around the wall onto the platform. His plan was to make his way to the baggage cart he and Frank had dragged to the center of the raised area. He'd use it as cover until he determined who shot who, and he hoped to get a bead on the location of Ballew. The gunfighter had to be responsible for the shooting. Will gritted his teeth. This meant someone helped him.

A knot of anger formed in the pit of Will's belly. This feud had gone too far. He would end it here and now or die trying.

"Don't move." Will froze where he stood. "Drop your gun." Will released his grip on the peacemaker and it fell to the wooden floor landing with a dull thud. "Hands over your head." Will raised his hands.

Colonel Carpenter appeared from his left coming from the direction of the train side of the platform. His blood shot eyes and face the color of red satin made Will nervous.

"Where's Ballew?" Will said.

"I shot him." The colonel grinned and giggled. Will realized he'd lost his mind.

"Did he shoot, Julia?"

The wild grin disappeared and the colonel's cool gaze shifted to his daughter laying on the floor not far away then back to Will.

He nodded. "Yes. Ballew. He killed my little girl."

Will nodded. "Good. He deserved to die then."

The colonel hesitated. As if he were a fish his mouth opened then closed. The once confident Union officer was gone. The hero of Appomattox had been replaced by madness. "Yes," he whispered, "yes he did. I killed him. I'm a hero."

"Absolutely, Colonel." There. Movement at the corner of his left eye. Will turned his head slightly and saw his deputy moving in crouching low to the floor. He carried a Winchester. His sky blue eyes were focused on Colonel Carpenter.

Suddenly he stopped and his eyes went wide. He'd seen Julia on the floor. He thinks she's dead.

"Huh, Colonel, how did Julia get shot?"

"He shot her."

"Who? Ballew?"

The Colonel nodded. "No. The devil came for her. She fell in love with a Montgomery. The devil came for her," he repeated again as if he'd made a decision. He turned away from Will. "I have to kill 'em. Kill 'em all."

Squatting to his haunches, Will grabbed his gun. He looked over to see Elbow straighten and point the rifle at the Colonel. He wore a scowl and his eyes blazed with hatred.

Will knew the look. He'd seen it too many times. "Elbow, no!"

The Winchester spat fire twice from the barrel and colonel fell forward to land hard with a sickening smack on his stomach. Blood quickly pooled around him.

Elbow ran to squat beside Julia. He set the rifle on the floor next to her body and placed his fingers on her face and gripped her hand with the other. "Darling!"

He sank to his haunches beside her and cradled her head with one arm supporting her shoulders. "She's breathing," he said his voice raw and sharp with fear.

A shaken Frank joined them from the telegraph office. "I'll get the doc." Will watched him disappear out the station entrance.

Will holstered his weapon then walked to stand over Elbow. "How bad?"

The deputy looked up at him muddy tears stained his cheeks. "I don't know."

Will stiffened and his heart beat faster when he heard a groan coming from the edge of train aide of the raised area.

He drew his gun and cocked the hammer then started slowly toward the edge. Once there he snuck a peek over the edge and withdrew out of site of whoever was by the tracks.

A Bad Day in Lunden Texas

A man lay on his back beside the train tracks. A man dressed head to toe in black. He had no hat and there was a splash of blood in the stomach.

Will hadn't seen a gun. He frowned and moved to stand at the edge of the platform his gun leveled at the man beside the tracks. Though he had never seen him this must be Steve Ballew.

With no evidence of immediate threat Will clambered to the side of Ballew. Trickles of blood trailed from both sides of the gunfighter's mouth. Evidently dying, but not yet dead, he signaled for Will to come closer. Will holstered his weapon then dropped to his haunches beside Ballew.

Ballew's breathing was labored and blood bubbled from his mouth. He whispered something but Will couldn't make it out. He took off his hat and leaned closer to the gunfighter.

"Please forgive me," Ballew whispered.

Will raised his head placed his hat back on his head and looked into the sad frightened eyes of the dying man. He patted the man's arm. "It's not up to me, Steve."

Ballew's body sagged as the last of his air escaped his lungs and his eyes lost the spark of life. He shook once a rattling sound came from his throat then he lay still his eyes wide, unseeing.

Will rose to full height and sighed. The man wanted absolution for a life lived badly, but he was no preacher. God would have to deal with him.

His job was to determine who killed the man. The late Colonel Carpenter claimed to have shot Ballew, but if his eyes were correct the evidence before him said otherwise. The belly wound was made by a rifle bullet. Large caliber. The size compatible with a Winchester.

This meant his deputy left his post at the jail, started the killing spree that led to the shooting of the woman he loved, and the death of her father. No doubt his reaction to seeing shot was equal parts love and guilt. Will shook his head. What a terrible mix of emotions he must be suffering.

Will turned away from Ballew's corpse and pulled himself up onto the raised area. He was grateful to see the doctor had arrived. He knelt down next to Julia his familiar black bag on the floor next to him. He was examining her wounds and sprinkling a white powder on her arm and had wrapped a bandage around her head. Frank and Elbow stood watching. Frank's eyes dropped at the corners and Elbow's were red from crying. His hands were trembling and his whole body was shaking.

Will joined them and watched the doc finish dusting Julia's arm and put away the container in his bag. After finishing the doc glanced up at Will. "She's hurt bad, but the wound on her head is more of a scratch than anything else." He sighed. 'I'll probably end up removing the arm, but there's not much I can do." His eyes flitted to Elbow. "If I don't when the gangrene sets in she will die. I seen it too many times."

Will placed an arm on Elbow's shoulder. "I understand, doc. I'm sure we all do."

"Right now though my deputy and I gotta have a little talk. Can you and Frank get her to his buckboard?"

Frank nodded. "Stanton came back. He'll help us." Will looked over his shoulder to see Stanton had indeed returned He caught Will's gaze and nodded, his face tight and his eyes grim.

"OK, thanks, doc. I'll check on Julia later."

He wrapped his fingers around Elbow's arm. "Let's go."

∗∗∗

Seated across the desk from him in the Sheriff's office Elbow fidgeted and he stared at the floor his hands worrying together in his lap. Will's fired him of course, but he wasn't going to arrest him.

He should have, but he wasn't going to. If he did it would start a war between Colonel Montgomery and himself. With all his ranch hands and his other sons Will would be on the losing end of the fight. No point dying for a lost cause.

Good thing Elbow and Julia were each the respective elders in their families. Clearly Colonel Carpenter had lost his mind somewhere along the way. As he'd done before he'd talk to Montgomery. He was the more reasonable of the two men so Will was confident the colonel would agree there had been enough bloodshed.

"I'm disappointed in you, Elbow, but if this is the way things have to be then fine by me."

"I'm truly sorry, Sheriff." He looked up. "Julia and I have agreed to get married. I'd like you to be my best man."

Will hesitated for a few seconds not truly believing what he was hearing then he chuckled. "Sure, Elbow. I'd be happy to."

A sense of relief washed over the sheriff. A marriage between the two families would mend the fences. At least someone would get their happy ending.

One Red Shoe

Operative Maddie Surefoot studied the shoe. It was sure a big one, at least twenty feet high. She'd never seen one like it. It looked familiar but she didn't know where she'd seen it before. All she knew for sure was she had seen this shoe somewhere.

Reaching inside her cotton suit jacket she pulled out her cell phone from her inside pocket and pressed the quick dial number for her section chief.

Barb Wallup's voice answered after one buzz at the other end.

"Maddie. What's up?" She sounded impatient. The boss must be having a bad day.

Maddie had already considered the summary of what she'd seen in her mind before she made the call.

"Hi, Barb, I'm at the scene now and it's exactly as reported by eyewitnesses."

Barb snorted. "I thought I'd seen everything." The chief paused. Maddie knew what was coming. "Any idea how it got there?"

The million dollar question. She had considered all possibilities, but nothing she'd thought of made sense expect one, and she didn't want to think about that. "No. There doesn't appear to be any reasonable explanation. So far."

"How about unreasonable explanations?"

"If you mean do I have a theory then, yes I might have one."

There was silence on the other end of the line. A pauses that spoke volumes. Barb Wallup was a practical woman who liked her explanations clean and simple. The Internal Secrets Bureau collected and hid many strange things from the general public, but everything had a rational explanation as far as Barb was concerned, no matter how fantastic.

"Ok, Maddie, try me."

Maddie sucked in a breath then let it out slowly. "I think this is the home of the woman who lived in a shoe, who had so many children she didn't know what to do."

There was a long pause. So long in fact, Maddie began to think Barb had hung up. Finally her chief asked, "You know what this means don't you?"

Maddie swallowed hard as her heart rate increased finally she said, "Yes. It means the giant is back in town."

***

Rednose the giant hadn't been seen in fifty years. If this was his shoe it meant he and his wife Brunhilda had been fighting again and the shoe had been tossed out of his kingdom on the other side of reality.

The land of unreality was the realm where there were giants, elf's, unicorns, and goblins, wizards and witches, and other creatures too terrible to dream of. The barrier between reality and unreality hadn't been breached since the beanstalk was cut down five decades ago.

Before she married her father, Maddie's mother, Irish McComb, had been an ISB operative. Irish had chopped down the beanstalk in time to stop the invasion of reality by unreality.

These days it would be simple if all the ISB had to deal with were vampires, alien invaders, or giant mutant insects, but an invasion from unreality? That was every ISB operative's worst nightmare.

One Red Shoe

Maddie's mother had saved reality barely in the nick of time, this time her daughter might not be so lucky. Too bad the cameras in those days were the size of a terrier and her mother had dropped hers while trying to climb down the beanstalk so fast or they'd have pictures of the giant and his castle. A lay of the land would be very useful of they were going to plan an adequate defense.

If the chief had her way they'd be planning a full scale preemptive assault rather than defense, but Maddie convinced Barb there was a better way than war.

Maddie stood on the cement walkway looking up to the porch that ran along the Victorian style house that was known to the world as the Shade Tree Seniors Residence. (STSR is the cover name for the Retired Spies, Saboteurs, and Terrorists Rest Home and Bingo Emporium. Apparently retired spies, saboteurs, and terrorists love to play bingo. Who knew?)

Maddie clipped the alligator clip attached to the top edge of her ISB identification badge to the breast pocket of her suit jacket. She took a deep breath then released it. She hadn't visited her mother for two months, so she'd have to listen to complaints about what a bad daughter she was.

She could hear her mother saying that just because Maddie was off on dangerous secret missions, facing death at every turn, didn't mean she couldn't find time to visit her elderly mother.

Since every internal organ in her mothers body had been replaced, and she'd been genetically enhanced in every way known to medical science, Maddie's mother was far from elderly. But nevertheless Maddie'd hear about her less than exemplary offspring skills.

She arrived at the front door of what looked to passersby as just another ordinary house on an ordinary street in an ordinary small town in America. What the world didn't know was behind this door was the most modern facility yet built to house the retired veterans of the secret wars of the past eighty years.

The door had no doorknob and there was no mailbox. The windows old fashioned wood framed windows on either side of door reflected the street and the yard but they were like one way mirrors. Whoever was on the other side could see out, but Maddie couldn't see what was on the other side.

Not that it mattered. She knew what was inside. She'd been here often enough. Just not lately, she thought.

Maddie reached inside her suit jacket and took out her id wallet.

She took out the proxima card she kept there and ran it over a section of wall next to the door.

There was a barely audible click and the door slide aside into the door frame. Mattie waited until the familiar mechanical voice spoke.

"Identify," it said. She'd never been able to determine if the voice was male or female not that it mattered, but intellectual games were something she enjoyed.

"Madeline Surefoot. Operative number 27, Internal Secrets Bureau."

There was a two second delay (yes, Maddie counted the elapsed time) then the voice said, "Identity verified. You may enter."

"Thank you." Though it was unnecessary to thank a machine Maddie had always considered politeness a worthwhile human virtue that separated them from the machines, and the beings in unreality who she considered non-human.

After she stepped through the open door it slide closed with a whoosh and a soft thud. Before her was the reception area with it's waterfall in one corner of the wide, carpeted lobby. The waterfall fell into a oval shaped pond bordered by a small forest of dwarf palm tress and tropical ferns and flowering pants.

The variety and splash of color and the bubble of water striking the small pond had always given Maddie a sense of inner peace.

She cringed inside when she saw Rocky Almost was working reception today. He was obviously on the telephone, speaking into his headset, his gray eyes focused on the flat screen monitor in front of him.

She and Rocky had dated for six months, until she discovered he had been living with another woman for over a year even after they began to date. She'd forgiven him, but it still hurt her to her core to see him. Ever since Rocky her trust of the male gender had never been at such a low level as it was now.

She approached the desk just as he ended the call. "Thanks and have a nice day." Rocky pressed a finger against the side of the headset.

Her mouth formed a tight smile as she tried to catch his attention. "Hi, Rocky," she said brightly.

He looked up from his monitor at her but he didn't smile. "Hello, Ms. Surefoot."

The use of her last name hurt Maggie worse than if he'd called her every four letter word in the dictionary. Whatever they had once felt for each was truly dead and gone. It was like they'd never know each other at all.

"I'm here to see my mother," she said, letting the smile fall away from her lips.

"Ok." He glanced at her id badge then placed a clipboard with an excel spreadsheet-style form and a pen attached by a string. There were columns for names, dates and times. He pointed with his index finger to the next empty space on the form. "Name date and time," he said, his tone dull.

"I know the drill," she said, restraining herself from snapping the words out. Given his hard exterior it seemed unlikely he'd be affected in the least anyway.

She completed the form then turned and walked away headed for the corridor than ran down the middle of the first floor. Behind her she heard him say, "Have a nice visit."

Maddie hesitated then rushed away, the knuckles of her right hand white from gripping the strap of her handbag that hung off her right shoulder.

She held back tears and her heart beat hard in her chest. She suppressed her emotions as she hurried down then wide tiled hallway past the recreation room, the theater and the gymnasium. Along the way she met several residents she knew.

Mrs. Campbell, a retired MI6 agent, Mr. Nahan, retired from Kenya's National Security Intelligence Service, and Mr. Yamanta, from Japan's Giant Monster Intelligence Bureau. She nodded at each one as she passed them. Mr. Yamanta had been living here for more than sixty years, but he didn't look a day over sixty himself. Maddie wish she knew the secret to his longevity.

Finally she arrived at her mother's room. She closed her eyes took a deep breath then released it slowly. After wiping her cheeks with the back of her hand she opened her eyes and rapped her knuckles on the door.

"Come in, dahlin," she heard her mother's distinctive southern accent come through the door.

Maddie pasted a smile on her face then opened the door. "Hi, Mom."

She froze when she realized her mother wasn't alone. A very elegant man stood next to her cream colored chaise lounger. He had a perfectly trimmed goatee that formed a sharp point on the end of his angular chin. Stuck in one eye socket was a monocle, and he wore a black velvet smoking jacket and perfectly pressed gray slacks. A fire engine red scarf surrounded his thin neck. It was tucked down the front of his jacket.

Her mother looked the same as always. Her dyed black hair was piled atop her head perfectly permed into tight curls. Upon seeing her daughter she leapt to her feet seeming to fly off the lounger, and threw her arms wide and ran at Maddie and wrapped her arms around her and hugged her tightly. Maddie thought about drawing her weapon.

"Maddie! My dahling girl! How long has it been?"

It had been what ten seconds and her mother had already started berating her for not visiting. "Two months, Mom. I'm sorry, I—"

Her mother startled her when she laughed brightly and released her. Her mother's eyes were bright and cheerful and she wore a wide smile on her face. Most importantly her eyes reflected her happiness.

Had her mother been smoking wacky-tabaccy, or was she drunk?

One of Maddie's eyebrows arched. There wasn't the tell-tale smell of marijuana smoke and she hadn't detected liquor on her mothers breath when she hugged her.

Hugged me? Maybe her mother had been assimilated by aliens? It had been known to happen. "Mom? Are you okay?"

It was then she realized her mother was dressed in a beautiful silk kimono that flowed around her body giving her the illusion of floating on air. Her mother laughed again then went to sprawl once again on the chaise lounger again. "No, no, dahling', I'm fine. I'm just in love is all." Her mother waved a hand at her. "Silly girl. Haven't you ever been in love?"

Maddie knew love, but she'd never seen her mother in love. Her father had disappeared when she was a little girl. Seeing her mother this way was a new and strange experience.

"Yeah, Mom, of course, but you haven't..." Maddie hesitated as her face grew warm. "You haven't been in love as long as..." Her voice trailed off. Had her mother loved her father? She had no idea, it wasn't something they'd ever talked about.

"Yes, muh dear daughter. I loved your father very much, but he's not coming back from the fourth dimension." She paused to grin at Maddie. "I'd like you to meet Lord Blacktoe, my fiancée."

The elegant looking man who'd bee silently observing them turned toward Maddie and held out one hand. "Charmed, Ms. Surefoot."

Maddie took his hand in hers and cringed inside. It was like shaking the tail of a dead fish.

"Pleased to meet you, Lord Blacktoe, so you wish to marry my mother?"

"Yes, Ms. Surefoot, I'm madly in love." Was he kidding? It was like he'd just told her he preferred marmalade on his toast.

Maddie offered him a tight smile then turned toward her mother. "Mother, I'm afraid I'm not here for a social call. There has been some trouble I need to talk to you about." She indicated Lord Blacktoe with a slight nod. "In private."

"Oh, poo, poo, dahling', Alfie is MI6. Retired, o' course. He's cleared to the highest level. Something' he calls the Official Secrets Act says if he tells anyone the Brits have to kill him. I'm shore he won't tell anyone. " Her mother batted her eyes at Lord Blacktoe. "Isn't that right, Alfie?"

The man's expression remained stoic he nodded his head ever so slightly, after his eyes had flitted between them. Did his expression ever change even when he was…Maddie pushed away the unimaginable image before it took hold in her mind. She shuddered and wanted to roll her eyes but managed not stop herself.

"Sure, Mom, no problem. Anyway, we found this big red shoe and—"

"The giant," her mother interrupted her.

As if she were a balloon she sagged into the cushions of the lounger and her features went slack as all color drained from her cheeks. "He's back," she whispered.

Maddie crossed her arms over her chest. "That's what we thought, until intelligence confirmed the bridge to unreality was still closed. There have been no other intrusions. At least that we know of."

Her mother's smooth forehead wrinkled. Sometimes Maddie thought with all the surgery her mother was starting to look younger than she did. "Then it has to be Jack," said her mother.

"Who?" Maddie's heart rate increased.

Her mother looked into her eyes, her features were taunt and her eyes seemed to bore into her daughters. "Jack, dear. Of Jack and the Beanstalk."

***

Maddie steered her Aston Martin DB9 into an empty parking stall that surrounded Beanstalk Park. The site where the beanstalk had been chopped down over fifty years ago was now a national monument surrounded by a park complete with picnic tables, a children's playground, and barbecue pits. It was a favorite spot for weekend family outings.

One Red Shoe

Since today was Saturday there were a myriad of Volvo station wagons and minivans occupying every other parking stall in the lot. Maddie's tricked out sports car was going to stick out like a frog in an onion field.

Maddie turned off the engine and got out. She kept her dark sunglasses on as she strolled toward the thirty yard wide stump. The stump was all that remained of the once awe inspiring beanstalk that ended in unreality.

There was a sign between two steel posts imbedded deep into the grass in front of the stump. The sign gave a short history of the stump and the beanstalk, leaving out the important secret details of how it had been cut down and who had done the task.

Maddie's mother had used a laser gun to cut the stalk down. Fortunately the area where the great stalk had fallen had been mostly uninhabited so no one was hurt when it crashed to Earth. A few cows, some sheep, and a few rabbits, had been crushed, and seismographs around the world had registered six points on the Richter scale, but the property damage had been minimal. The ISB had paid off anyone who submitted a claim, a fact even Congress didn't know about. Black ops money was way off the books, and an operation like that cost huge amounts of cash.

Maddie sauntered up to the fence guarded the stump so the children wouldn't climb it and to prevent teenagers from carving their initials into the green stalk. Kids. Maddie shook her head and smiled to herself.

Her mother explained that the Jack who'd managed to transport the red shoe wasn't the original Jack. Apparently original Jack had been a very busy boy in unreality.

He had dated most of the female children of the old-woman-who- lived-in-a-shoe-who-had-so-many-children-she-didn't-know-what-to-do and the giant. She and the giant had sired several hundred children.

Before he left unreality, Jack, had fathered a lot of children. Apparently, the male children were all named Jack Junior. As stupid as it sounded it made sense when you had so many children you didn't know what to name them.

Maddie scanned the park from where she stood by the fence. Children, dogs, mom's and dad's, everyone enjoying the sunny warm weather. Maddie had to push away the sadness that gripped her. Her family had never enjoyed simple pleasures like a day the park. Her family had too often been apart separated by continents or dimensions or where ever the latest secret mission took them.

She'd never had any intention but to join the family business when she was old enough. Her mother once explained that being a spy was in the blood. Secret agent work was a family tradition going to back to the days when an Italian ancestor worked uncover as a Roman agent. Maximus Gallus Surefoot accompanied the Hannibal expedition. He sabotaged Hannibal's plans to conquer the Roman empire.

Maddie frowned as her eyes settled on a man across the park.   Near a stand of pine trees. He looked out of place. He was short, in fact so short, she suspected he was a little person (she decided she wouldn't mention it). He wore a black and white pinstriped suit and on his head he wore a straw hat titled to one side at a cocky angle. Most notably he was alone, like her.

She wondered what he was doing here in the park. His eyes were covered by dark sunglasses and he appeared to be studying her. The most direct approach seemed the most practical.

She approached the little man her eyes warily flitting side to side looking for threats. The man didn't move. She continued when there were no obvious threats.

"Hello," she said as she came up to him.

"Hello, Operative 27." His voice had a surprisingly deep baritone quality to it.

Her eyes narrowed. "Do I know you?"

The corners of his curled. "No. But Chief Wallup does. She sent me."

Maddie's stomach muscles tightened. Obviously Barb didn't want to tell her about this contact. "Oh? Who are you then?"

"I'm with R&D." He paused, turned around and started to walk into the trees. "Follow me. I have something to show you."

Maddie hesitated. Walking into an unknown forest with a man she didn't know was reckless if not irresponsible. As a precaution Maddie reached into her suit jacket and pulled out her ASP semi-automatic pistol. She didn't want to shoot anyone but she would if cornered. The ASP was a good weapon for close quarters like this forest of trees.

The little man was quick so she was breathing hard when she arrived in the clearing. What she saw made her breath catch in her throat and she froze where she stood.

A two story balloon floated above the mashed down grass in the clearing. It was tethered to the ground by ropes tied to wooden stakes pounded into the ground. Red, yellow and blue stripes covered the balloon.

The air was thick with the smell of rotting leaves and cut grass.

"Operative 27, come over here."

Maddie took in a breath and looked in the direction of the man's voice. Beside the balloon stood the man. He'd doffed his sunglasses revealing sapphire blue eyes.

"What's the balloon for?" Maddie asked as she holstered her gun beneath her jacket.

"I'm going to take you to unreality in this balloon." Maddie looked at him the surprise registering on her face. The man held out a business card.

Maddie took it and read his name was Mike Oz, PhD, Mac, Eng. "So you're the Wizard of Oz?" Maddie smirked. "Nice try, pal."

The little man laughed. "No, of course not. I'm a scientist and I'm going to take you to unreality in this balloon."

Maddie eyed Dr. Oz with one eyebrow cocked. She'd seen a lot of strange things, a balloon that would take her to unreality wasn't outside the realm of possibility.

"I thought the portal between reality and unreality wasn't accessible."

Dr. Oz shrugged. "It isn't, for most people."

"Do you have a permit?" Permits were required to travel to unreality. Maddie had never seen one but she knew it was a requirement.

"Uhhh…not exactly."

"Not exactly, huh? That's what I thought." Maddie turned to walk away. "I'm so outta here."

"Hold on, Ms. Surefoot." Maddie stopped. "Chief Wallup wants you to go. That's why she sent me to see you. It's dangerous, against the rules, and filled with adventure. Most importantly if we do this its very likely we'll save the world."

Maddie spun around a wide smile pasted to her tanned features.

"Now that's my kind of mission. Let's get this balloon in the air."

***

After three hours of flying time they arrived in unreality. The balloon floated on the warm air. Giant birds, with what looked like forty foot wing spans, floated along side them their wings spread in order to ride the updrafts.

Maddie spotted the giant's castle first on the horizon the twin stone towers piercing the puffy white clouds. The same birds that now floated in the air around them had constructed nests along the castle walls and some sections of wall had collapsed reminiscent of a child that had lost baby teeth sporadically.

Had something happened to the giant?

They soon arrived at the castle and Dr. Oz managed to find a safe place to land amongst the stones that fell and landed haphazardly along the base of the castle walls. The castle and the surrounding area looked deserted.

The forest had encroached the park-like area that bordered the castle land, and the grass had grown waist high in sections.

What bothered Maddie was evidence of a battle. Large sections of grass had been burned black and some trees in the nearby forest were charred, some having collapsed, or the tree trunks were shattered before they were blown apart.

Who in unreality had the nerve and the firepower to go up against the giant?

What she didn't realize was the grounds were imbedded with sensors and their arrival had been noted.

Half an hour later a green army jeep broke from the forest. Three men rode in the vehicle with one man standing in the bed of the jeep manning a machine gun. Maddie watched their approach with trepidation. Who's army were these guys with?

All of the men wore reflective aviator glasses and the passenger had an unlit cigar between his teeth.

The men's rippling biceps were bare, tanned and covered in scars.

The passenger had the butt of an automatic rifle resting on his thigh the barrel pointed to the sky.

"Hey, there, little lady," said the passenger over the squeal of the jeeps brakes as it stopped in front of them.

Maddie crossed her arms over her chest and shifted her weight to her left leg. "Name's ISB Operative Madeline Surefoot, not little lady." She reached into her pocket and pulled out her identification wallet and flashed her credentials.

The man chuckled and removed his sunglasses to reveal a warm brown eyes a woman could get lost in. "Sorry, Ms. Surefoot, name's Jack. I'm in charge of this military zone."

Maddie arched an eyebrow. "Really? You're Jack? Well, then, Jack, tell me what's happened here."

The smile dissipated from Jack's rugged features. "War. Death. Blood."

"Sorry? War? With whom?"

Jack got out of the jeep. Maddie was impressed. He was over six feet tall with a wide chest and muscular arms. He moved with the confidence and strength of someone who could handle himself. He threw the cigar to the ground then crushed it under his boot heel. "You've heard of the old woman who—"

"Yes. I know who she is. What about her?" Maddie was growing impatient. Barb wanted her in unreality for a reason, and it wasn't to play footsie with some soldier boy, as appealing as that might be. Jack was clearly handsome and just the type that would break her heart.

The guy probably had hot and cold running blondes back at base camp.

Jack eyed her with a sly grin on his lips. "My grandmother is leading the defense of unreality."

"Revolution? Against what? Fairy's and goblins?"

"Not exactly. You see—" The stone wall behind them exploded raining them with bits of rock and mortar. Smoke and dust filled Maddie's nose and mouth

"Com'on!" yelled Jack. "We have to go."

He jumped into the jeep while the man with the machine gun began firing sporadically into the forest. Maddie ran to the jeep with Dr. Oz close behind her.

Jack motioned for her to sit in his lap and Dr. Oz to climb into the back. Maddie considered protesting but another explosion to her right made up her mind. She sat across his lap. He wrapped one arm around her waist to keep from falling as the jeep jerked and started to drive in a zigzag pattern across the open park land.

Maddie locked her arms around Jack's neck and held on as the jeep swayed side to side and bounced across the open field.

The drivers features were grim and his arms were stiff with tension as he struggled to keep the jeep from rolling over due to the sudden increase in weight.

An explosion near the front left bumper sprayed them with dirt. The driver made a sharp turn to the right to avoid the crater created by whatever ordinance the enemy was using. Maddie felt like she'd lose her lunch. She tasted bile at the back of her throat.

The driver drove like a man possessed (which is entirely possible in unreality) until they rounded a cliff. With a wall between them the explosions stopped but the driver kept zigzagging.

After twenty minutes they arrived an encampment surrounded by guard towers on the four corners. Teams of men and women stood in the guard towers scanning the plains that ran away toward the granite cliff they'd left behind them. The jeep pulled up to a guard house and gate and came to a stop, the brakes squeaking loudly.

"Sergeant Jack Bean, Recon Unit 6." He indicated Maddie with a nod. "This is ISB Operative Surefoot. The guy in the back is Dr. Oz, ISB R&D."

The guard nodded. "Thank you, Sergeant. You may pass."

Maddie started when she heard the familiar sound of a bolt being cocked on a fifty caliber machine from somewhere above them.

She glanced at Jack. He offered a twisted smile. "The war hasn't been going too well. Creates itchy trigger fingers," he explained simply before the jeep bounced beneath them and they roared into the compound.

They stopped in front of a forest green canvas tent. Maddie extracted herself from Jack's lap and everyone piled out.

Jack faced his three soldiers. "You guys go have a shower and get some hot chow. Meet me back here at 1900 hours."

"Will do, Sarge," said the driver. The other two men merely nodded their expression unreadable.

Jack turned toward Maddie and Dr. Oz. "I'll take you to see my grandmother."

Maddie nodded and attempted to smooth her rumpled suit with her hands. A few stray hairs fell across her eyes. She blew them away only to see them fall back. She stole a glance at Oz and saw he was trembling, badly shaken by the wild ride.

She patted his shoulder. He looked at her and she smiled at him.

"That's what field work is like pretty much all the time. Fun, huh?"

Oz cleared his throat. "Yeah. Fun."

Jack snorted obviously amused by Dr. Oz's reaction. "The general is in this tent," he said, nodding toward the tent the jeep was parked in front of.

They followed Jack inside the tent to find a gray haired woman with the weathered features of someone who'd spent too much time in the sun. The lines on her face reminded Maddie of aged leather. The old woman was seated behind a large ornate oak desk. Her brown eyes looked up from the paper she'd been reading when they entered. When her eyes settled on Jack her weathered features broke into a wide smile. She got up and moved quickly around the desk. She wrapped her arms around Jack and hugged him to her.

After several seconds they broke their hug and she took a step back and gripped his arms with gnarled hands. She gazed into his eyes.

"I heard there was an attack?"

Jack grinned. "No, worries, Gran. Pete got us outta there okay. He's one heck of a driver."

She released Jack from her grip and dropped her arms to her sides. The smile on her face disappeared, only to be replaced by a deep frown.

"Yes, but it means they're close. Too close." She walked around her desk and sat down. "Who are they?"

Jack chuckled. "Sorry. This is ISB Operative Surefoot and Dr. Oz. We found them at Rednose's castle and decided not to leave them to the hostiles."

"For which I and Dr. Oz are very grateful," said Maddie. "General, I must know, what is going on?"

The general gazed at Maddie with dead eyes and her features darkened. "Why were you sent to unreality?"

"With respect, General, I believe I asked a question."

The general leaned forward in her chair and laid her arms flat on the desk. "We are at war with the giants and others, and we don't have a lot of time. Now tell me, why are you here?"

Giants? Plural. There were more than one of them? Oh well, in for a buck in for twenty. "Because of a red shoe that landed in reality."

Maddie frowned. "But what about Rednose? He's a giant."

The general's features softened and her eyes became bright with tears. "He died. When my husband refused to join in with their war they killed him…" Her voice trailed off and she wiped at her eyes with the sleeve of her uniform shirt. Maddie had seen such pain before and decided she'd drop the obviously painful subject.

She cleared her throat and shifted her gaze to Jack.

"Is the shoe drop your doing, Sergeant?"

He nodded his mouth a grim line.

The general sighed and eased back in her chair. "We're losing the war, and Jack thought your world might be willing to help."

"What makes you think that?" Maddie frowned at Jack. He grinned sheepishly and her heart fluttered. He was way too handsome for his own good.

"Because, Operative Surefoot, if we lose, your world will be next."

***

Maddie was excited when the general asked Maddie to work with Jack on strategies and plans for counter attack. It would give her chance to know him better.

They stood side by side looking over a waist high table made form sawhorses and plywood. A large map of the battle fields had been spread out on the table and blue and red pins had been used to indicate the coordinates of both sides. Maddie's frown grew deeper the longer she stared at it and realized what it was telling her.

The enemy had broken through their defensive lines in several places. This had resulted in retreating battles between the army of the shoe and the giants and their allies the dwarfs (yes, the irony is not lost on me) and the ogres.

Most of the fairytale creatures were with them. A entire village of cookie people and pie makers had declared themselves neutral. So far the enemy had honored their neutrality, but Maddie knew it was only a matter of time before they too were drawn into the war.

Jack stood beside her smelling of soap and cigar smoke. Right now an unlit cigar stuck out from between his gritted teeth. At least he washed. "So what do ya think?" he said.

"You guys are pretty much screwed."

Jack grunted. "Yeah. I know. Any ideas?"

"You mean other than heading for the hills?" She shook her head and emitted a sharp laugh. "But since your pretty much surrounded and the enemy is closing in that ship has sailed."

"So we surrender and hope they don't execute us?"

"Nope. We ask Dr. Oz to build us some weapons. Non-lethal weapons."

She glanced at Jack and saw the arrogant smile had faded and his features had paled. Good, she thought, I threw him a curve ball.

She turned to face him. "Non-lethal weapons will preserve the balance in unreality. If the giants and ogres are all gone then who will rise up and take over?"

She arched an eyebrow. "You? The general? The wild unicorns?" Her eyes narrowed. "Or maybe the wizards? We certainly don't want the wizards to take control. That would be very bad and for your world and mine."

Jack's eyes narrowed and he stroked his stubble covered chin with strong fingers. He looked so handsome she had to stop herself from shivering. "I see what you mean." He dropped his hand to his side, his palm now resting off the butt of his pistol in the holster around his narrow waist. "But can Dr. Oz build enough weapons, fast enough to turn the tide of, " with his left hand he swept an arc over the map, "this."

Maddie nodded grimly. "I think we have a month. Dr. Oz can and will do it." Her voice lowered to a whisper. "Or we all die."

***

Maddie rubbed the eye pieces of her gas mask before she stole a look over the wall of sandbags. There they were. The giants were moving across the open field toward their position. The looked warily and slapped their hairy palms with their tree sized wooden clubs.

In the last month Dr. Oz had constructed several new classes of weapons for the locals that had taken out several hundred giants and ogres. The fairies and shoe elves had worked night and day to turn out non-lethal bubble guns, and shock cannons, and giggle grenades. These weapons had turned the tide of war in their favor. Maddie was relieved the enemy hadn't changed tactics when the new weapons were deployed and continued to be dependant on their brute force alone.

All that remained of the giants, dwarfs, and ogres army were five giants. The rest of their army had been incapacitated and captured. It was up to her and Jack to take out these last few.

Maddie slipped down once again behind the wall and reached for the box of giggle grenades. She glanced at Jack in his gas mask and they shared an awkward smile.

These giants were going to get a big surprise when they got within range. The incoming giants were causing the ground to tremble beneath the defenders. The earth shook more violently with each deep thud of their massive boot steps as they drew ever closer.

Finally, when Maddie thought they were close enough, she issued the order her troops had been waiting for with a loud yell. "Now!"

She stood up with a grenade in her right hand, Jack did the same. They each pulled the pin, counted to three, then threw the grenades into the path of the oncoming giants. They dropped down once again behind the sandbags and covered their heads with their arms.

There was a loud bang and the invisible gas dispersed. Maddie heard the giants coughing and the first giggles started. Soon they were laughing uncontrollably. After ten minutes elapsed she heard the five giants fall with thuds so loud she had to cover her ears, her teeth chattered, and the impact made her heart skip a beat.

Maddie began to laugh herself as did Jack. She and Jack had become close and for the first time in along time it seemed she could trust a man again.

Jack turned out to be a kind and gentle man with great passion, and he was a good kisser. But if he was going to win her heart he would have to give up the cigars and shave once in awhile. The latter not too often, of course, she kind of enjoyed the feeling of his stubble on her skin.

After the mop up crews had these remaining giant's secured, and locked in the holding pen to await trial for crimes against unreality, Maddie met with General She-Had-So-Many-Children-She-Didn't-Know-What-To-Do.

They each had a cup of warm mint tea in front of them. "So, my dear, when are you going back?"

"Back?" Maddie sipped her tea.

The general shrugged. "To reality. To your job. Your old life."

Maddie shook her head. "I think I'll stick around for a while."

The general arched one eyebrow. "Oh? Is it my grandson?"

Maddie chuckled. "Yes, partially. But I don't think these giants were alone. I think someone helped them, or incited them. They seem to be puppets of a greater power."

"You may be right." The general's tired eyes dropped to peer at her tea cup. A small smile drifted across her pale lips. "I was hoping you'd make an honest man of my grandson."

Maddie lifted her cup to her lips and peered at the old woman over the rim.

Before she took another sip she said, "That could be a distinct possibility.

Hard to believe this had all started with one red shoe. Maddie was certain Barb would understand her reasons for staying. She only hoped her mother would.

Big Hairy Deal

For once I wasn't in the office when our future four-legged client bounded passed me snarling at screaming civilians. At the time I was concentrating on squeezing a grapefruit at Mo's Fruitland on Bleeker Street, near the office.

My office is located on the third floor of a three-story, mold-covered brick walk-up above Bleeker Street in the city of Vancouver. And not the pretty-multi-cultural-Mecca-Vancouver by the sea you're thinking of--the one on the west coast of Canada. My Vancouver is the one sucked into the dark, gloomy alternate reality where paranormal is normal.

Big Hairy Deal

Today is a day like most days. I'm squeezing fruit watching a crazed vendor swinging a broom in self-defense at a werewolf and I know I have to do something about it. It's my job.

With my partner we own and operate a private detective agency. We solve problems in the neighborhood. Unusual problems. No, not plumbing or electrical problems, those are someone else's problem. We deal with the who-ya-gonna-call kinda problems.

In an alternate universe I used to be an agent for the Legal Investigative Protection Service. Yes, I am the original Woman From L.I.P.S. Impressive I know, but when Matt and I were accidentally sucked into a space-time portal we ended up here where the L.I.P.s doesn't exist. A girl with my skills has to have something to do so naturally we became PI's.

Matt Butcher, former zombie, and my some time boyfriend, is my partner in our little two-person agency, Abby-Normal Investigations.

Our motto is: We take on any case no matter how weird, how supernatural, how small, how big, or how much you want to pay. Justice is our middle name.

My middle name is actually Mabel, but I hate it.

I introduce myself using only my first and last name. "Armstrong, Aloha Armstrong. Private Dick" has a nice ring to it. Aloha Mabel Armstrong? Yuk.

Russ Crossley

As far as I'm concerned my middle name is as big
a secret as the combination on the suitcase with the
nuclear launch codes.

Anyway, Matt and I handle the cases the cops are
too scared to, or the ones they have no idea how to.
Zombies, vampires, midgets (some of my best friends
are midgets), swamp monsters, and all sorts of alien life
forms are our traditional client base. Let me tell you
aliens are the worst tippers. Anyone got change for a
Zelbot drudge?

Yeah sure, every once in a while a real person walks
through the door, but they're usually looking for the
can.

So today, as I'm squeezing the grapefruit, this
werewolf suddenly appears and starts tearing up the
fruit stand and threatening to eat the customers. Since
I'm a lot like Batman (other than the shoulder-length-
copper-red wavy hair, knee-high-spike-heeled leather
boots, leather mini-skirt, and mid-rift-barring-too-
tight tee we are exactly the same), in that I carry every
sort of utility item in my purse. Naturally, I come to the
rescue.

I pull a werewolf biscuit from my purse and quickly
have this werewolf understanding who's the alpha. In
fact, soon the beast was on its back whimpering like a
puppy and I'm scratching its belly.

It doesn't take long before there is the inevitable shape shift and a naked woman lay at my feet and I'm scratching her belly. Ok, I know this sounds weird (and it is), but in this universe weird is my business.

I stand. "You okay?"

She blinks, with her arms and legs still in air in that aren't-I-the-cute-little-puppy position, then said, "Yeah, I think so." A frown creased her brow. "But I'm not sure."

I sense there is more to this woman's story, I just need to dig a little deeper. I need Matt.

***

Once back at the office I make her cup of green tea for our prospective client while Matt gives her blanket to cover herself. She's shivering by now, not a surprise given it rains most of the year. I glance out the window overlooking Bleeker Street in time see a flash of lightning brighten the gray overcast sky. Really? Does it have to be gloomy all the time?

Our office is located downtown, in the seedier section of the city, in a building way past its prime. Not that it's going to be here much longer.

Foreign developers bought blocks of the seedier parts of downtown a few years back, and have built several towers worth of condos in the midst of the cesspool. For eight hundred grand you get a closet with a great view of another closet with a great view. Did I buy one of these expensive shoeboxes? Yeah, right, I may work with the undead but I'm not brain dead.

Anyway, the woman, her name is Lizzie Harris, turns out to be an accountant for a mad scientist bent on world domination.

Why anyone would want to dominate this world is beyond me. The place is such a mess, and you'd have to spend all your time running around fixing stuff. Like I'm the handy-woman type? I don't think so.

Matt, with his calm demeanor, is, as usual, able to elicit information Lizzie doesn't realize she even knows. Square jawed Matt, with his wavy brown hair, intense hazel eyes, and aura of confident strength makes most women weak at the knees. He's beautiful and he's mine. A least for now.

In the dark days before Zombie Away, Matt suffered from zombieitis. I often wonder if his inner calm comes from his days as a zombie. He seemed so care free when we first met. Maybe if you know you're going to turn to dust soon you have a different outlook on life. I'm no shrink so what do I know?

Our on-again, off-again relationship suffers because he has no sense of humor. He's so darned serious all the time and it drives me nuts. He says I'm too sarcastic to be a good detective. It's our sore point.

Lizzie tells us the mad scientist has been cooking the books and stealing from his investors. Who knew mad scientists had investors?

I sit half listening to her explanation of his embezzlement scheme, thinking about my hair appointment this afternoon, not particularly caring about any of this, (you invest in the evil scheme of a crazed genius what do you expect?) until she says he also applied for some government research grants under false pretenses.

"I think you just threw us a bone," I blurted silencing Matt and Lizzie.

Lizzie looked at me slack-jawed and the corners of Matt's mouth curled slightly then dropped back into the familiar grim line. He'd never admit it but I just made him laugh.

"Is that a crack?" Lizzie said indignantly.

Oops. Time for damage control. "Huh, sorry, no not at all." I tried my best let's-be-pals smile but she glared at me. Her angular features were pinched like she'd sucked on a lemon. Werewolves can be touchy about their inner wild child.

"What I'm referring to is the part about your boss ripping off the government. I don't like that." I lowered my voice. "I mean, I really don't like that."

Lizzie shriveled deeper into the worn wing chair and gripped her teacup tighter causing the color to drain from her knuckles. I swear I saw fear in her eyes. A frightened werewolf is just pitiful.

I may have gone too intense, but then sometimes you have to let the client know you're not all sweetness and light. It's especially important, when you're a hot looking babe like me, that people see your serious side.

Matt gazed at me and gave me the slight nod he does when he's telling me to cool it. He rolled his shoulders beneath his perfectly tailored double-breasted suit, then shifted his gaze to Lizzie. "Sorry about her. She gets a little carried away." Her paused to clear his throat. "What she means is the government will pay us to find out more about your boss' embezzlement scheme."

Lizzie grinned at him like a schoolgirl on her first date. I suppressed the urge to gag, and crossed my arms over my bosom, determined to keep quiet.

Matt continued. "What's your boss' name."

"He's quite mad you know?" Matt nodded. "His name's Tres Zero."

Big Hairy Deal

***

The Zero's had been haunting us since we started this agency. In fact even before that when we stopped the father, Arnold Zero, from stealing the formula for Zombie Away. Then we stopped his son, Uno when he threatened to turn the whole world into zombies.

A Google search confirmed Tres Zero is the illegitimate son of Uno Zero and the bearded lady from the Dingaling Brothers Circus.

Yup, we're up to our necks in zero's, again.

This simple case of embezzlement had suddenly turned into a race against time to stop another Zero from taking over the world.

My heart pounded in my ears and my blood coursed through my veins. It's s days like this when ya know this crime fighting gig just never gets old.

***

We arrived at Castle Zero, situated at the end of a windy, dirt road atop Mount Seymour overlooking the city, just as dusk fell. When you live in a place where weather is an issue let me tell you dusk falls hard.

The night was as black as the inside of a cookie jar. Not that I know what the inside of cookie jar looks like, but a girl can dream, even when she's always on a diet.

Matt's driving. The '74 Pinto rattled and wheezed its way up the winding road up the side of the mountain. Pelting rain bounced off the roof of our rusting hulk of a car. We stopped outside the ten-foot tall front gates guarding the long gravel driveway. The Pinto sighed as if were relieved to get this far.

No kidding, me too.

It often occurred to me our car might be haunted, which wouldn't be surprising, but that investigation would have to wait for another day. We had tax fraud and a take-over-the-world case going at the same time so our plate was full, thank you very much. No room for the small stuff.

Lizzie told us she'd pay mucho dollars to get the goods on her boss. And when we had the evidence of fraud we'd turn it over to the government. They pay handsome rewards for stuff like that.

I'm hoping it's enough so Matt and I can take the big vacation we always talked about—or rather, I talk about. He just listens and nods.

And then there's the whole saving the world thing. That's just icing on the cake.

I mean we're talking about a mad scientist, not a rocket scientist, how serious could it be?

The Pinto's four cylinders chugged, and the fan belt whined and squeaked, as I stared through the streaky windshield at the gates. Along the tops of the steel bars were images of hissing gargoyles and grinning fairy's with mouths full of sharp teeth. Not the most inviting thing I'd ever seen, but not the worst either.

There were those smiling clowns of Slashing, Montana. I shivered. That's an image I'd rather forget, but never could.

"There's an intercom," Matt said, with a nod of his head at the stonewall next to the gates. I squinted into the darkness. Sure enough through the shimmering rain I saw a square black pad with an oval shaped lemon-yellow button affixed to the wall about knee height from the ground.

"Oh, you've got to be kidding." This Zero is a chip of the old woodpile. The button being where it is means he's a little person. It seems in the Zero family all the fruit hangs close to the ground. "Not too far to fall, I guess," I muttered.

"What?" said Matt.

"Nothing. It's a joke."

He nodded, his face hard as steel. "You gonna get us in?"

I flipped a coin on the drive here to determine who would get out if there were a gate. I lost. I looked down at my expensive leather boots, then at the muddy road, then at Matt. I think he knew there'd be a gate.

I swung the car door open, then pulled my plastic raincoat over my head, and ran to the wall. Mud squished under foot and the smells of the surrounding fir and pine trees filled my senses.

Before I pressed the intercom button I noticed there was what looked like a coin slot on the panel, I hadn't noticed from the car. Odd. Never seen a coin slot on an intercom before. I shrugged and pressed the button.

I waited while rainwater dripped off my coat all around me, and shuffled my feet so my precious leather boots wouldn't sink any deeper into the sucking mud. After what seemed like forever, a gravel crunching voice came over the intercom.

"Yeah?"

I'd practiced my pitch all the way here. I knew Matt grew tired of listening when he started saying every one was pitch perfect, even though some were just stupid and off key.

"Hi, we're from Publishers Habitat Sweepstakes. We have a check for Dear Occupant." I took my finger off the button.

Girl, when your wit is on it's really on.

There was a slight pause then the voice said, "Mr. Occupant doesn't wish to be disturbed. Go away."

I pressed the button again and laughed, "No, wait. Please. That was just a little sweepstakes humor we use round the office. Actually, I have a big fat check for a Mr. Tres Zero. Would Mr. Zero be at home?" Again, I released the button.

I could feel it in my bones, this was gonna work for sure.

There was another pause, only longer this time, then the voice said, "Put fifty cents in the slot and come up to the house. Greta will meet you." The tinny speaker crackled then fell silent.

Yeah, baby you are sooo smooth.

It was then I realized I didn't have any coins on me, and for sure not in my I'm-so-cool-I'm-tiny-purse back in the car. I glanced at the slot. It didn't look like it took bills. I looked to the car with its fading headlights and sagging suspension.

I hoped Matt had exact change.

***

We came back in two hours. Thankfully, the gas station we passed at the bottom of the mountain was still open.

The snag-toothed attendant even pumped gas for us so we could get the right change we needed. Ever try to pump exactly two dollars and fifty cents worth of gas? It 'aint easy.

After we got back I first buzzed the house to let them know we had returned, then slipped the coins into the slot.

I ran to the driver's side of the Pinto and climbed in as the tall gates slowly opened on squealing hinges.

Once past the gates the Pinto groaned and popped as it crunched over the gravel driveway. I winced as a rock pinged off the undercarriage. The car had to last another year, at least until I made the final payment.

Finally, we stopped on the circular driveway in front of the two-story ink-black mansion. There were stone steps leading to a heavy oak door with a gargoyle knocker. A row of twenty-foot marble columns stood on either side of the steps holding up an overhang off the sloped roof. The mansion reminded of Scarlet O'Hara's in Gone With the Wind crossed with the Addams Family house.

We got out and walked up the steps to the door. I was grateful for the overhang; it kept us out of the rain.

Matt tipped the edge of his fedora to let the excess rain fall off, (I really love when he wears his hat.

It makes him look all Sam Spade.) then used the gargoyle knocker to announce us. As the echo of the thump, thump dissipated the door began to swing aside. They must have oiled the hinges recently because it did so soundlessly.

I expected the interior to be a gloomy as the exterior, but was surprised to find a well-kept foyer with a polished wood floor, a maroon-navy Persian rug, and a rose wood side table with a matching chair beside it. On the table was an antique lamp that cast a soft glow over the woman who greeted us.

A gentle smile played across her thin lips. "Hello, Mr. Butcher and Miss Armstrong," she said, gazing at us over her reading glasses in a way reminiscent of a school marm. She was short—no more than four-foot eleven—with grey hair pulled into a tight bun atop her oval-shaped head. Her navy and red paisley dress, that ran past her knees, hung loosely on her small frame and on her tiny feet she wore plain black slip-on shoes.

"I'm the doctors housemaid, Greta."

"Hello, Greta," I said, deciding in the interests of time to use the direct approach I'm best known for. "We're here to see the doc. We hear he's planning on taking over the world."

A puzzled frown formed on Greta's forehead. "I'm sorry, dear but I don't know what you're talking about. Dr. Zero is trying to help people."

Matt interrupted before I could rebut the old lady. "Sorry, Greta, my partner gets a little carried away some times." He glanced at me and raised an eyebrow.

Oh, I get it. Good detective. Bad detective. I nodded but scowled at him to add to the illusion I was angry. Which I actually was, but since it enhanced my role as the bad dick I decided to play along.

Greta smiled at Matt in that creepy, cougar-like way. I swear Matt could charm the pants off Ann Coulter on her worst day.

He continued. "We've come a long way to see Mr. Zero." He patted the left breast of his suit jacket. "We have the check."

"Yes, of course. I'll take you to his laboratory." She turned and started to walk away. "Right this way."

She led us through the quiet house filled with more antique furniture, Persian rugs, the woods floors polished and gleaming. We passed a grandfather clock that chimed the half hour. The black arms on the brass face told me it was eleven-thirty already.

Finally, she led us into a massive library with floor-to-ceiling shelves filled with hard cover books. I stared at the old lady. Is she kidding?

The secret entrance to a mad scientist's laboratory in the library is so old school. It's a cliché.

She walked to another door at the other end of the room then used a brass key; she withdrew from the pocket of her dress, to unlock it. She swung it open and inside was the laboratory complete with a work bench with racks of test tubes, and humming machines for I-don't-know-what, and a man who could only be Dr. Tres Zero.

His lab is on the first floor, not the dusty basement? Sometimes even I can be wrong.

As I suspected, Tres Zero was a little person with slicked oil-black hair, a neatly trimmed goatee and mustache. He wore a gray vest under his white lab coat and white running shoes on his feet. To me he looked more like a miniature version of Sigmund Freud than a mad scientist, but looks can be deceiving.

"Hello," said Zero with a grin, his thumbs hooked off the pockets of his vest. A chain from a pocket watch hung across his belly between the vest pockets. "Can I have the check, please. I have a lot of work to do before midnight."

Midnight! That must be zero hour. (Com'on, you know someone had to say it.)

"What happens at midnight?" said Matt, his hazel eyes casually scanning the laboratory.

"You two and the others will be my slaves," Zero said, like he was ordering a skinny latté with a twist.

My stomach muscles tightened. We were about to take a trip on the crazy train. Good thing Matt's the boy scout of our little agency. He always comes prepared.

Glancing at the old woman I saw her being to shape shift. The old lady gave way to a snarling, flesh-eating werewolf, and I'm fresh out of werewolf biscuits.

Matt reached into his suit jacket and pulled out his .45 automatic. Without warning he turned the gun on the old lady-werewolf and shot her twice. Once in the chest, the other in the middle of her forehead. The first shot stopped her in her tracks, the other blew out the back of her head scattering her brains across the lab. The bullets slammed her backward and she landed hard then shifted back to her human form. It wasn't a pretty sight.

"Silver bullets?" I said.

Matt shrugged. "Of course."

In the commotion Zero ducked under the laboratory bench and disappeared into a trap door in the floor.

Suddenly gas jets lit up with blue and red flames along the parameter of the walls.

Big Hairy Deal

Like all mad scientists Zero had a self-destruct-when-discovered-obsession so the house and all its contents, including the evidence of fraud, was going up in flames. If we wanted to avoid going up with it we needed to leave right now. There'd be no time to search the house.

We may have stopped Zero's evil plan for world domination, whatever it is, but our payday was gone.

***

The next day we sat in the office with our feet on top of our desks discussing the Zero case, hoping the next client would soon darken our door.

"What do you think Zero was up to?"

Matt shrugged then took a sip from his Mickey Mouse coffee mug. "Werewolves I'd say."

"Werewolves?"

"Yeah, ya know a big hairy deal."

I looked at him and his features were as serious as ever. "You know you just made a joke, right?"

He shook his head. "Nope."

I sighed. "Some day you're gonna slip, and I'm gonna be there to laugh my butt off."

Grind Manor

AMANDA DARK STOOD ON THE cracked cement sidewalk in front of the crumbling manor house where the taxi had dropped her with one hand buried in the pocket of her wool coat shivering in the cool fall air. In the other hand she held a worn brown leather satchel containing two heavy duty flashlights, three wax candles, a small case with nail files, a set of various size screw drivers, and a box of wooden matches. Like the girl scouts she was always prepared.

Golden, crimson, and burnt orange leaves danced in the westerly breeze. As if stirred by some unseen hand, the leaves tumbled across the weathered blacktop of the deserted street in front of her. Ignoring the leaves her gray-green eyes scanned both directions of the street.

The air smelled of fall rot mingled with the lingering odor of charcoal from trash fires in the surrounding neighborhoods.

A shiver travelled through her body. She wished one of those fires were here right now. She wasn't what people describe as lean, but she wasn't fat either so she wasn't a fan of the cold. She liked to think of herself as a medium build sun worshipper.

Phil certainly seemed to enjoy snuggling with her on the sofa on cold nights watching old movies. She shifted her feet back and forth to try and keep her circulation going. There were no cars in sight. Where could he be?

No calls...her cell phone in her coat pocket beeped. Ah, ha.

Taking the phone out she peered at the small screen and saw Phillip Swann's office phone number. She uttered a soft curse under her breath as she keyed the green answer button, then brought the phone to her right ear.

"Yes, Phil?"

"Uhhh, hi, sweetie. I know you're mad because I'm late but a client dropped in unexpectedly. I'm so sorry. Please forgive me?"

Amanda smiled to herself. Phil sounded so cute when he begged.

And a lawyers hours were often as bad as a paranormal investigators she really couldn't be mad at him. She'd just let him think she was annoyed, it might get her a free dinner. She arched an eyebrow hoping it might reflect in her voice.

"How long?" She couldn't conceal the amused edge in her tone. A quick glance to the glowing horizon told her sunset was less than ten minutes away and unless Phil had wings there was no way he'd be here in ten minutes.

"I'll be there in twenty."

"You better." Cutting the connection without a goodbye hoping by doing so to add to his incentive to hurry. Amanda dropped the phone into the pocket of her coat. Her brow wrinkled. Ever since they met on Hook Island where she'd helped Phillip clear his family name they'd been seeing each other regularly.

It wasn't exactly a boyfriend-girlfriend relationship by the traditional definition but they had been spending a lot of time together for two people that weren't dating. Of course since he started getting requests at his law practice where her unique services were the perfect fit, they had worked together on a number of cases. It was as if some unseen force were bringing them together for some as yet undefined purpose.

A soft mew at her feet made her look down and sure enough Scars sat on his haunches gazing up at her with his black eyes, his black tail tipped with white flicked back and forth. The ghost of the 18th century pirate captain's cat had been her contestant companion since returning from Hook Island. She didn't mind actually. Scars made good company, and he didn't need food or a litter box so he traveled well. In other words the perfect pet for someone who didn't want a pet. Of course, a ghost cat that can pass through solid objects made him handy to scout out an old house or tomb for her.

She chuckled to herself. Scars had been her ghost scout cat since he decided to adopt her. Just like living cats, ghost cats adopted you not the other way around.

Phil couldn't see Scars only she could. This new ability of hers (with Scars help) to survey a house or tomb before they entered seemed to impress him Phil even more. He already knew about her empathic abilities, another handy feature for someone in her profession.

She dismissed the idea of her and Phil being more than friends. They enjoyed each other's company, a few snuggles, and a few kisses, but that's all.

And they were both unattached so how did a little harmless flirting between consenting adults hurt anyone? She certainly didn't have any plans to sleep with him, though he did stir her juices like no one had before.

Clearing her thoughts of such things she turned her attention to the long abandoned manor house beyond the steel fence guarding the perimeter of the over grown yard. Ancient, gnarled and knotted trees dotted the property reminding her of arthritic old men twisted by time and age. The once lush gardens were overgrown by weeds and choked by vines. The lengthening shadows gave the vines the appearance of invading snakes twisting and grasping the remaining bushes and gnarled trees as if choking the life from them. An occasional bird call cut through the swoosh of the strengthening breeze.

It was a decidedly creepy old house sitting in the middle of a neglected property. The brick framed house rose three stories The rows of windows on each floor facing the street were dark the brick facade tinged green by moss. The house had a sagging wrap around porch and an ornately carved front door with a massive door knocker shaped like a dragon with it's mouth open as if spitting fire.

Grind Manor

From her research, Amanda learned the house had been abandoned in the 1960's after the death of the family's only daughter, sister to the two male twin brothers. One brother hired Phil's law firm to represent him in an estate dispute with his twin. They were all the children of the recently deceased, Lord and Lady Grind who fled to America after an insurrection in the African nation where they'd lived for over twenty years. The couples lives ended in a private plane mishap outside Paris two years ago.

According to spookrumormill.com these days Grind Manor had one lone occupant. A ghost. Specifically the ghost of the sister. Her name was Priscilla. She died of pneumonia at the age of twenty-three.

Bertram Grind hired Phil to find a copy of another will hidden somewhere in this house. He'd claimed the house was haunted and when he tried to enter on his own the ghost chased him off. He'd been too afraid to enter ever since.

Phil contracted Amanda to clear the house of the dead sister's spirit so Bertram could search the house to find the wayward will.

While it wasn't really her business, Amanda suspected the will in question differed from the one his twin, Maxwell Grind, had presented to a probate judge which bequeathed him a substantial portion of his parents, the Lord and Ladyship Grind's very affluent estate holdings.

According to newspaper reports, Bertram hadn't been cut out completely, but the amount reported was no where near the inheritance of his twin brother. Phil only told her Bertram disagreed with this assessment of his situation.

I may be just the paranormal investigator but I can read between the lines like anyone else. Bertram's slice of the old family pie must be miniscule compared to his brother. In fact she suspected the difference is measured by how many zeroes there are behind the words many, many millions.

Her thoughts were interrupted when a taxi pulled up to the curb and stopped. Phil shot out of the back seat stepping onto the sidewalk and waved to her, his handsome features split by a wide smile. Every time they met he seemed pleased to see her as if they hadn't seen each other for a long time.

"Hi," she called her cheeks were warm even in the cool breeze. Phillip always made her heart rate rise and her breath come harder.

One day she would act on this, but today was not the day. There was work to be done first.

The trees surrounding the old house had begun to stir swaying in the rising force of the wind. The branches brushed each other like the ancient arms of old men. Amanda shivered and pulled up the wool collar of her coat holding it tighter around her neck. She hoped it didn't snow this early in the fall or getting cab to this end of Boston would be an almost impossible challenge.

Phil moved to the curb side of the cab and leaned in the window of the passenger side handing the drive a few bills. "Keep the change," she heard him say.

She didn't hear the drivers reply, but the light on the roof of the car lit up and he sped away. She watched the yellow and black car until it disappeared around a corner at the end of the block.

"Whew. It's cold out here," said Phillip who joined her with his hands buried in the pockets of his ankle length leather overcoat. "Why didn't you wait inside?"

"I like to survey the outside before I enter a haunted house," Amanda explained. "Besides I didn't want the client to think I'd walk off with the will if I tripped over it by accident."

He eyed her up and down. "What's with the runners?"

"In case I need to make a fast getaway."

Phil smiled. "OK, but let's go inside. It's wayyyy too cold out here." He approached the steel gate and pulled it open with one gloved hand. The hinges shrieked but the heavily rusted gate swung aside surprisingly easy. The orange crust covering the steel shattered and rained down on the path like rusty snow.

Ever the gentleman, Phil entered first then held the gate open for her. Amanda cast a shy smile as she walked past him. His eyes sparkled at her in the gathering dusk as she went by. Her eyes drifted from his to the windows on the second floor. A flash of white light made her stop. She peered at the windows. The light didn't reappear. As expected they'd already attracted some spectral attention.

Her brow wrinkled and she arched an eyebrow. The house had been abandoned for decades, she doubted the electricity had been left on. "I think I saw our ghost," she said.

"Really? Where?" Amanda pointed to the darkened windows on the second floor. "I don't see anything," said Phil.

"I saw a light in one of those windows." She locked eyes with Phil.

"I don't think the electricity's on, do you?"
He shook his head. "Let's go." After she approached
the wrap around front porch she stopped to open the
satchel. She took out the two flashlights, handing one
to Phil, she clicked hers on. The brilliant white light
cut through the growing darkness illuminating the
front porch. At the edge of the beam Amanda spotted
movement and brief flashes of small yellow eyes. This
was immediately followed by the furious sound of tiny
toe nails scratching the boards as rodents clambered
over each other to escape the sudden intrusion.

None of this surprised her. Many an old house's
occupants were of the vermin variety once the humans
vacated. At least the living humans. It often occurred
to her there had to be reasons why the rats and mice
weren't afraid of ghosts and ghouls. Do they know
something we don't?

Amanda stopped as she tested the boards on the
first of three short steps leading from the weed infested
footpath to the porch. It seemed solid enough. "One at
a time, Phil. Just in case," she added nodding at the gray
weathered wooden planks underfoot. He nodded.

Turning away she carefully walked up the three
steps until she stood on the porch. The boards creaked
but appeared strong enough to hold her weight. Their
combined weight might be another matter.

She raised one hand to signal to Phil to wait. Just as she did she froze, her empathic ability detected something — something that bothered her. At the edge of Amanda's awareness she sensed a distinct feeling of grief. A surge of sorrow so deep it shook her to the core of her being.

Something bad, something very bad, had happened here. She sensed pure anger from the ghost. It seemed to be an all consuming anger, and in her experience this isn't a good state for a spirit. She didn't sense any evil presence behind it, just a deep sadness leading to frustration. No wonder Bertram had fled the house in panic. If she didn't have her experience with ghosts such feelings could be very frightening.

(I'm reading panic into Phil's sketchy description of Bertram's flight so don't take me literally. I have no idea how he flew — or should I say ran —from the house? Phil really has to learn to be more exact in his descriptions of events. I require as much information going into an unknown situation as possible if I'm to do my job properly.)

She started walking again until she stood at the front door. The finish on the door was peeling but still appeared solid. The dragon shaped knocker was made of solid brass with an oval shaped loop of brass affixed to the knocker just below the dragon's head.

Grind Manor

The brass was severely tarnished from the weather. Not surprising given it had been here since Grind Manor was constructed in 1947.

Amanda thought about using the ornate door knocker but dismissed the idea as silly. Only the dead were home and from what she'd sensed they weren't going to be all that welcoming to the living.

She hesitated. This was the first time since she and Phil joined forces she felt failure had such a high price. Why? Something nagged at the back of her mind, A darkness. It was as if her empathic ability were warning her. She shook off the feeling. In her job she'd seen a lot of scary stuff, why would this job be any different, but she was having difficulty shaking off her growing sense of unease.

Gripping the brass door knob she turned it and discovered the door was unlocked. Glancing over her left shoulder she nodded to Phil who still stood on the steps waiting to walk forward. She didn't want him to break an ankle if the boards on the deck gave way. She heard a click as the door latch disengaged then used the flat of her other hand to push the door in. It swung on rusty hinges creaking in the silence. It occurred to her the birds making crying noises from the ancient trees on the overgrown property had ceased since she entered through the gate.

Weird may be her business but this was too weird.

Scars skittered by her legs as he disappeared into the interior. She wasn't concerned about him. After all he was dead already so what was the worst that could happen to him?

Peering through the murky air at the interior beyond the door the dust floating in the still air supported the claim the house had been abandoned for a long time. Streams of waning sunlight cut through the murky windows splashing spotlights of light across the dirty tiled entry in the foyer. In the shadows she could make out a small table set against the short wall at the base of the staircase. On the table rested a half-moon shaped lamp with a dusty cloth shade covering the light fixture. Cobwebs draped across every surface and hung off the curved banister guarding the wide staircase that swept upward to disappear into the darkness.

Amanda stepped inside and waved for Phil to follow. She noticed he had donned leather gloves. Was he concerned about leaving fingerprints or touching something icky? Probably both, she mused. She wished now she'd remembered to bring hers.

After pulling out the other flashlight she flicked the switch on the casing and the powerful halogen light came on easily chasing the darkness away.

Using the beam as her guide she scanned the foyer and saw the two French made rosewood chairs coated in thick gray dust one each on either side of the table where the lamp sat.

She swept away cobwebs that hung like a curtain from the ceiling with the satchel as she moved farther into the room. The heavy scent of must and mold filled her nose and mouth. Suddenly Scars appeared running toward her from her left his glowing emerald eyes reflecting by the beam of light from the flashlight. She was glad for Phil's inability to see the cat, if he had he'd have probably been freaked out. Scars ran everywhere he went so his abrupt and hurried reappearance didn't startle her in the least.

Scanning her surroundings she saw three sets of twin oak doors exiting off the foyer. One each left and right and one at the bottom of the staircase. She picked the one at bottom of the staircase to investigate first. She set the satchel on the table beside the lamp. She had considered going upstairs to find the room with the window facing the front of the house where she'd spotted the glow but decided she first better see if they could find the library or study. They were here to find a will and that room seemed the most likely location. The ghost could wait, for now.

"Let's find the library," said Phil from behind her echoing her thoughts.

She grinned to herself. They were so often in sync it scared her.

She moved to the doors she selected and turned the brass doorknob. She swung the door open and shone the light inside. Through the floating dust she saw the room was indeed the library. A thick Persian rug covered the floor. The gold, royal blue and crimson pattern had a thick coat of dust obscuring its once ornate pattern. An oak desk the size of small car sat to one side of a floor to ceiling stone fireplace. Amanda stepped inside batting at the cobwebs with her free hand. Phil came in after her closing the door on its squeaky hinges.

"Do you think there's a safe somewhere?" Amanda asked her eyes focused on the framed painting on the wall behind the desk. Two walls contained floor to ceiling bookshelf's.

"Yeah. For sure," breathed Phil his voice low. "This place is really something."

"It sure is, Phil, but where would the safe be?" A faint odor of whiskey and stale cigar smoke lingered in the air. To her this signaled the room had been used frequently in the past for after dinner business back in the day.

"Uhhh...I suggest the painting?" Phil swung the beam from his flashlight over the painting. The subject was a sallow-cheeked man with a gray beard and dark, serious eyes. He was dressed in 18th century clothing of a type she'd seen in many of these old houses and the tangled mass of his hair was comprised of black and gray strands. A metal plate affixed at the bottom edge of the wood frame read, Lord Grind 1744-1799.

Phil moved behind the desk and ran his fingers along the fame's edge. His brow wrinkled and he next pulled the frame away from the wall with the fingers of his free hand. The painting wasn't hinged like in the movies. He directed his flashlight behind the painting then pulled it away from the wall as he looked behind it.

After a second or two he released the painting. It thumped against the wall. "No safe," he said simply.

He ran his flashlight around the room scanning the books on the shelves. Amanda directed her beam to the floor and studied the carpet. She didn't know what exactly she was looking for but when Scars appeared through the carpet she knew where the safe was hidden. He wagged his tail at her and mewed softly. She smiled to herself. "I found it."

"Really? Where?"

Directing her beam at the carpet where Scars had appeared she said, "Under the carpet in the floor."

***

It took them forty minutes to move two heavy oak side tables, an ottoman, and two leather wing chairs against one of the book cases so they could lift the carpet away to in order to access the trap door in the floor. The carpet was surprisingly heavy but between them with sufficient sweat, grunting and groaning, they managed to left up one corner and fold it back so it was out of the way. It formed a mountain of heavy, thick carpet to one side of the desk.

After they caught their breath, Amanda trained her flashlight on the trap door and saw it had a key lock. Now where was the key? She arched at eyebrow at Phil. He rolled his eyes and grunted. "Why is it never easy?" he asked what she was thinking.

"I'll look in the desk drawers," she said. "You check the books for a hollowed out one."

"Really? Sounds a little Hollywood-ish to me."

She grinned. "Who do you think movie folk consult when they need the spooky details about those old houses?"

Phil chuckled. "Oh? My girlfriend knows Steven Spielberg, eh?"

Amanda stiffened. Phil used the G word. Now was not the time to discuss this. "Just look for the key, smart guy."

He offered her a lopsided grin and his eyes sparkled. Before she could react he looked away and walked to one of the two book cases. She kept her eyes locked on his back as he began running the palm of one gloved hand over the books. Shaking off the effect his words has caused, she shook her head then let out the breath she'd been holding in. She started clambering over the carpet until she was behind the large desk.

In the middle was a large single drawer which she tried first, but as she'd expected it was locked too. Things were not exactly going to be easy. Then again too often she was forced to take the harder road.

Grunting from the excretion she struggled back over the thick mountain of folded Persian carpet she checked with Phil to see if he'd found any keys. He hadn't so she went the foyer to retrieve her satchel from where she left it on the table. Walking back into the library she sighed as her eyes fell over Mount Persian.

Gritting her teeth she once again climbed over the carpet until she was behind the desk.

Setting the satchel on the desk she opened it and took out two nail files. One was larger than the other, but she didn't know which would work better so she decided to try both. Picking up the shorter of the two from where she'd placed them side by side on the desk she stuck the tip in the desk's lock and twisted. The tip broke off in the lock.

Amanda fought the urge to throw the broken nail file across the room. She took in a deep breath then let it out slowly.

She stiffened when a cold breeze suddenly washed over her. The hair on the back of her neck rose. "Miss Dark?" said a breathy voice. A woman's voice by the timber.

"Yes..." she whispered.

"Open the bottom drawer on the left," instructed the voice.

Amanda licked her dry lips and opened the drawer as instructed. "What next?"

"Pull the middle drawer toward you." Amanda hesitated. "It'll open. I saw my father open this drawer many times."

As Amanda assumed the voice had to be Priscilla Grind, the ghost of Grind Manor.

She wrapped her fingers around the edge of the drawer and pulled, sure enough it slid open, far easier than she thought it would, considering how long it had probably been closed. The lock had obviously been a ruse to fool would be robbers or curious people like her.

The pencil tray in the drawer had a few paperclips, two pencils, a pen, and a large steel key. She smiled to herself. "Thank you, Priscilla," she murmured.

"You're welcome, Amanda."

Amanda's her cheeks grew cold as the blood drained from her face. She was having a conversation with a ghost. After she meets Phil she starts to see ghosts now she's having full blown conversations with them. What's next tea and cookies with the spirits? Maybe her meeting Phil wasn't an accident after all?

Picking up the key to study it she decided it was about the right size for the trap door lock. She stuck it in the pocket of her black slacks then made her way back over the Persian hill while carrying the satchel. She checked the first item off on her mental mission checked as completed. She was confident the copy of the will would be in the safe beneath that trap door. At least she hoped there would be a safe. All that was left now was to clear the house of Priscilla, help her on her way to her next destination.

She found Phil, his suit jacket thrown across one of the wing chairs they had moved earlier, standing on a step ladder testing the books on the higher shelves. "Phil, I have the key," she announced triumphantly.

Phil glanced over his shoulder at her. His face was pale and drawn she suspected from frustration and weariness. His broad shoulders slumped and he nodded. He stepped off the step ladder and joined her gazing down at the trap door. She squatted and stuck the key in the lock. The key turned and there was an audible click. She glanced at Phil and grinned. He nodded his eyes sparkling with excitement.

The trap door had a steel handle resting in a perfectly shaped hollow imbedded in the steel so it lay flush with the edge and wouldn't protrude. Amanda pulled the handle out and up. The door didn't budge.

Phil dropped beside her. "Let me try," he offered.

Amanda let go of the handle and Phil grabbed it. He pulled hard but again it didn't budge. Would this day never end?

Phil's brow wrinkled. After rolling up the sleeves of his powder blue dress shirt he gritted his teeth then grabbed the handle with both hands. His cheeks puffed out and she watched him count silently to three then he began to pull hard, the muscles in his strong arms straining.

His face became red as pomegranate and his arms trembled. He kept pulling until finally with a loud cracking sound the trap door flew open sending him off balance backward.

"Hey!" He landed hard on his tail bone, the air rushing from his lungs. He lay gasping trying to draw a breath. Dust flew in the air around him the musty smell stronger than ever.

"What you seek isn't beneath the trap door," said the woman's voice.

Amanda looked around using flashlight to scan the library. They were alone. But the voice had been right before. Weird she didn't see Priscilla. Ever since Hook Island Amanda had gained the ability to not only sense emotion but she'd been able to see the ghosts. The feeling of confidence she felt emanating for this unseen spirit was strong and clear, but was it really Priscilla or a deceptive poltergeist playing the nasty games they were known for? She had been fooled a few times before, not that she wanted to dwell on those dark events.

"So where is it?" she said mentally crossing her fingers.

"Pull out the middle drawer of the desk, underneath you'll find a envelope taped to it."

Amanda sighed. Back over the mountain once again. "It's not in there," Amanda said.

Her voice sounded heavy and dulled by a lack of energy. Closing her eyes she sagged back on her haunches overwhelmed by the feeling of total defeat.

"Where?" said Phil simply.

"Taped under the middle drawer of the desk." She nodded her head toward the mountain of carpet. "I can't go over there again..." Her voice tailed off. Amanda stiffened as fingers brushed her left shoulder. Phil's touch sent shockwaves of passion through her. You pick the worst times, girl.

A calmness came over her. "I'll do it," she heard Phil say. She wanted to open her eyes and watch him but she didn't want the feeling he'd planted in her to end. Instead she followed him by the sound of his shoes, the sigh of the carpet compressing under his weight as he clambered over it. Finally the sound of the drawer being opened, then silence.

"I got it!"

Her heart beat faster. "He loves you," said the voice of the woman.

"Priscilla?" Silence. No response.

She heard the scuff of his shoes as Phil returned over the pile of carpet. She shot to her feet as her eyes flew open. Phil walked up to stand in front of her. His dirt smudged face was split by a wide grin. In his right hand he held a manila envelope.

Before speaking Amanda threw her arms around Phil's neck and shoulder s and dragged him into a passionate kiss. She held him for several seconds and sensed no resistance from him. Good, he felt the same way about her as she did for him.

Finally she released him and they parted. "What was that all about?" he said. "Not that I'm complaining."

Amanda chuckled. "I'll explain later. Show me what you found."

Phil held up the envelope and opened the flap on one end and drew out two documents. "Bertram was right there was another will, but he neglected to mention his sister had a child. A girl, born in 1967. The parents names are interesting." he handed her the birth certificate first.

Amanda eyes went wide when she saw the baby had the same last name as both her father and her mother. Priscilla was the mother while her brother, Maxwell, was listed as the father. Creepy.

Phil next handed her the will he'd found with the birth certificate and the baby listed a Melanie Grind was an equal beneficiary of the Grind family estate.

"So where is this Melanie Grind?"

"I don't know but I intend to find her. This revelation will probably invalidate the new will arranged by Maxwell. He can't cut out an heir to the estate. Ultimately a judge will determine who gets what. I suspect this was what Bertram was after all along."

He took the documents from her and stuffed them back in the envelope. After retrieving his suit jacket. He placed his flashlight in the satchel then picked it up and touched her elbow to lead her out of the library. Amanda used her flashlight to light their way.

When they were in the foyer and about to go out the front door he suddnely stopped. "What about Priscilla?" he asked.

"Don't worry about her, Phil, I'm sure she's fine." In fact during her review of the documents she sensed Priscilla had exited this world for good now she knew her child would receive her rightful inheritance. She'd found her peace at last.

The truth did indeed set you free.

She sensed not only had this investigation been successful but her and Phil's relationship was about to take on a new dynamic. Amanda Dark has a boyfriend. I like the sound of that. Something soft brushed her leg.

Grind Manor

Looking down she saw Scars had joined them. His glowing eyes looked up at her as he purred. Her ghost cat appeared to concur with her view.

The adventure in Grind Manor would indeed be a memorable one.

About the Author

International selling author, Russ Crossley writes science fiction and fantasy, and mystery/suspense as well as their various subgenres.

His latest science fiction satire set in the far future, Revenge of the Lushites, is a sequel to Attack of the Lushites released in 2011. The latest title in the series was released in the fall of 2013. Both titles are available in e-book and trade paperback.

He has sold several short stories that have appeared in anthologies from various publishers including; WMG Publishing, Pocket Books, 53rd Street Publishing, and St. Martins Press.

He is a member of SF Canada and is past president of the Greater Vancouver Chapter of Romance Writers of America. He is also an alumni of the Oregon Coast Professional Fiction Writers Master Class taught by award winning author/editors, Kristine Katherine Rusch and Dean Wesley Smith.

Feel free to contact him on Facebook, Twitter, or his website http//:www.russcrossley.com. He loves to hear from readers.

He has sold several short stories that have appeared in anthologies from Pocket Books, St. Martins Press, at Smashwords, Amazon, and other e-retail sites.

With his wife, romance author R.S. Meger, he owns and operates a small press publishing company, 53rd Street Publishing. The company began in April 2011 and now has over one hundred e-book titles and a number of print titles, with more planned in 2012 and 2013.

He is a member of SF Canada and the Greater Vancouver Chapter of Romance Writers of America. He is also an alumni of the Oregon Coast Professional Fiction Writers Master Class taught by award winning author/editors, Kristine Katherine Rusch and Dean Wesley Smith.

To find a complete listing of his work check out his website http://www.rghart.com, http://russstory. blogspot.com.Razor's blog can be found at http:// razorandedge.blogspot.com

Feel free to contact him on Facebook or Twitter. He loves to hear from readers

Other Novels

Attack of the Lushites
Revenge of the Lushites
My Zombie Prince
Antique Virgin
The Fire In Their Hearts
with R.S. Meger (from Champagne Books)
Zomopolis
The Last Serial Killer

Short Stories
Countdown
Shoeless Moe
Round Up At The Burger Bar:
The Story of Trixie Pug, Parts 1, 2, 3, 4, 5, 6, 7, 8, 9
Five Minutes
Blossom Queen, Barbarian
The Secret
The Family Line
End of the Flies
Death by Magic
The Penguin Sleeps With The Fishes
Only The Worthy
Hero For A Day
End of Empire
Strange Bedfellows
Big Business
A Perfect Crime
The Wise Guy and The Pirates
In Search of the Perfect Cup
T.I.N. Men

The Legend of G and the Dragonettes
The Incredible Mr. Fix-It
Lock Stock and Barrel
Divided Loyalties
Cave of Wonders
A Family Empire
Until We Meet Again
Dragon Rising
Solitary Man
The Keel Mountain Conspiracy
Angel on My Shoulder
Heroes of Old
The Great Bicycle Race
Tikka's Big Day
"My Partner the Zombie" —
Hungry For Your Love Anthology
(St. Martin's Press)
Big Hairy Deal
One Red Shoe
A Bad Day in Lunden Texas
Bloody Betty, Queen of the Pirates
Mirror Image
Dangerous Waters
Cape Disappointment
Boomerang
The Watcher of Wayburn Street
The Apprentice
Drip!
A Beautiful Friendship and The Parrot of Doom
Robine's Diary
The Christmas Club
Loose Ends

Splatter Pattern
It Takes Two
Lexicon
Replacement Parts
Sidekicks
Lost Stories
Time and Space
Survivors
Neighborhood Watch
Unnatural Immortal
Rum Runner's Lounge
It's A Small Galaxy
A Shattered Man
Betrayed
Replacement Parts
Clubhouse Heroes
Sounds That Angels Make
Muggins Rules – originally published in Fiction River
Volume 12, Risk Takers

Anthologies
Tales of Urban Fantasy
Five Tales of Bizarre Detectives
Tales of Mystery and Suspense
Tales of Weird Fantasy
Spies, Detectives, & Heroes
Tales of Twisted Crime
Tales of The Unexpected
Tales From Space
10 by Russ Crossley
Round Up At The Burger Bar: The Story of Trixie
Pug,Parts 1- 5 The Beginning

Worlds of Science Fiction and Fantasy
More Tales of Mystery and Suspense
Ladies of the Jolly Roger
Justice Served
Love Stories
Ladies of the Jolly Roger with Rita Schulz
The Adventures of Razor and Edge:
Five Tales From The Quirky Detective Team
An Unexpected Journey
On Edge
Thrilling Adventures
Total War

Non-Fiction
The Writers Tools - The Synopsis

Also available from 53rd Street Publishing

Aloha Armstrong, The Woman from L.I.P.S returns in an exciting new adventure. Her mission: to go undercover as sheriff of Zomopolis, a domed town where incurable zombies are kept until a cure can be found, to discover the fate of the previous sheriff who went missing under mysterious circumstances.

She soon discovers a town filled with secrets, people who might not be who they claim to be, and a deadly conspiracy than threatens to destroy humanity. Handsome diner owner Hanson Braddock, a man with his own secrets, offers his help but can she trust him?

Surrounded by possible enemies Aloha must face a decision that will change her life forever.

Will Aloha save the world from certain doom or is this her final mission?

The book may be purchased from your favorite online bookseller or ordered from your local book store.